21 Nights with Billionaire Boss: A Romantic Suspense (Magic Island Book 1 - Chance)

Summer Hunter

Copyright © [Year of First Publication] by [Author or Pen Name]

All rights reserved.

No portion of this book may be reproduced in any form without written permission from the publisher or author, except as permitted by U.S. copyright law.

Contents

1. Chapter One — 1
2. Chapter Two — 12
3. Chapter Three — 23
4. Chapter Four — 32
5. Chapter Five — 41
6. Chapter Six — 51
7. Chapter Seven — 61
8. Chapter Eight — 70
9. Chapter Nine — 76
10. Chapter Ten — 85
11. Chapter Eleven — 94
12. Chapter Twelve — 104
13. Chapter Thirteen — 114
14. Chapter Fourteen — 124
15. Chapter Fifteen — 134

16.	Chapter Sixteen	143
17.	Chapter Seventeen	153
18.	Chapter Eighteen	162
19.	Chapter Nineteen	171
20.	Chapter Twenty	180
21.	Chapter Twenty-One	189
22.	Chapter Twenty-Two	198
23.	Chapter Twenty-Three	207
24.	Chapter Twenty-Four	216
25.	Chapter Twenty-Five	224
26.	Chapter Twenty-Six	233
27.	Chapter Twenty-Seven	245
28.	Chapter Twenty-Eight	253
29.	Chapter Twenty-Nine	259
30.	Chapter Thirty	264
About the author		273

Chapter One

Maddie

I'm unpacking my suitcase when it tumbles out—Todd's notepad containing scheduled plans for our trip. I snatch it up and toss it across the spacious, primly decorated room. It slams into the wall and tumbles into the trash can.

Satisfaction doesn't fill me as I expect. Instead, a bone-deep weariness forces me to drop onto the fluffy bed and bury my face in my hands.

"You're supposed to be having fun, Maddie." I run shaky fingers through my thick brown waves.

Massaging my scalp always helps me feel better but right now, it just reminds me that it used to be Todd's job until he fucked another woman.

I gulp back a tear and release a slow breath. Two weeks have passed since I caught them together. I should be getting over it by now, but it still stings. Five years down the drain. Just like that. Maybe I wouldn't feel so lost if our breakup didn't coincide with losing my job. Yep, both on the same day.

Now, at 29, I have no love life. No job. And I'm on vacation in Magic Island knowing that when I get back to the city, I've got lots of work to do. Where's the fun in that?

My phone rings and I grab it from my purse. It's Nat, my BFF, who gladly took Todd's spot as my plus-one on this trip.

"Where are you?" The background is filled with cheering.

Nat is already at the garden party we spotted on our way in. It's open to everyone and she swore she'd get down there once we checked into the resort hotel.

She's fast.

"I'm just setting aside my stuff."

"Mads, what are you doing? Did you come all the way to THE Magic Island to clean up? You'll fix your clothes whenever. Come down and enjoy the party, dude."

"But—"

"No excuses. You only fix your closet when you are sad and I'm not letting you mourn Todd for a second longer than necessary. And that second expired two weeks ago. Come out now or I'm coming for your perky ass."

"Fine." I throw my head back with a groan. "I'll be out in a minute."

"See you soon."

I toss my phone onto the bed and stuff the closet with my clothes. The only pieces left are a bikini and a sheer flower-patterned gown.

Because I was so sad I couldn't leave the house, Nat did the shopping for this trip. I should have known letting her go alone was a wrong move. While Nat thinks the littler clothes, the better. I'm the opposite.

I glance at the closet doors and shrug. Anymore dilly-dallying and Nat would find her way up here and hassle me. Best to get dressed and get down instead of looking for something else to put on.

I slip out of my basic underwear and fit into the bikini. I stop in front of the long mirror. My jaw drops. Of course, it's a size too small.

"Natalie..." I grumble.

My phone starts to ring again. Sure she's calling me to make sure I'm on my way, I slip into the sheer gown. It's soft on my skin, the sleeves reaching to my wrists and the hem flowing around my feet. And it's showcasing every inch of my body.

My phone's consistent buzzing irritates me. "Fine! Sheesh. I'm coming down."

I grab my purse and phone and head out. Thankfully, no one's in the hallway to see me looking this dressed down. By the time I get to the party, everyone there would be similarly dressed and I won't be the odd one out.

I take a second to appreciate the art on the wall and the plush carpet lining the hallway.

I fill my lungs with much-needed oxygen and exhale. Leaving the hotel room already has me feeling better. I'm going to enjoy myself. I press the button on the elevator and wait.

My phone rings. Again.

I grab it from my purse, ready to lay into Nat. But it's a number that isn't hers. I know this because first, there's no caller ID and secondly, I have this number stored in my memory because I used it to reach my ex for five years.

The elevator door slides open but I'm too busy glaring at my phone screen, my thumb hovering over it, indecisive. It would be great to pick up and give my ex a piece of my mind. But I also don't want to ruin my day talking to him.

"Are you coming in or what?" a deep baritone voice says.

I look up and my mouth pops open. A literal god stands in the elevator. He's wearing a light gray suit with a white shirt underneath. The open collar reveals deep olive skin. Pushing out a breath, I look up to meet eyes that are a dark blue, almost black. Even the atmosphere around him carries the same energy and I debate entering the elevator. Not because I'm terrified.

No, I'm worried about what I'd do locked in a space with this man. For reasons unknown to man, a chill races through my body and I know it's only him that can warm me.

His eyes assess me too, and they grow darker. Probably because I'm nearly naked.

The elevator doors begin to slide together. He stops their smooth glide with a firm hand.

"Come in," he stresses.

Yeah, right. That's what I'm supposed to do. I step forward, just over the threshold of the elevator doors, and stop there.

There is no way I'm drawing closer to him.

The doors start to move again. This time, they close and then we're descending. I feel a tug and then—

Twaarrpp.

What in the world?

I look down and my heart jumps into my throat. The entire lower half of my dress is gone. And I'm standing in a public space with only my bikini bottoms and half of a dress.

Shame heats my cheek. I glance up and the man's looking at me, a slight sneer on his lips. I press my thighs together but there's no way to hide myself. I won't be able to go back up until we get down. I have to risk running into other people.

Shit! What do I do?

I inch my way to the corner of the elevator and glue myself to the wall. Maybe if I make myself as small as possible, no one would notice me.

It doesn't take long before the elevator stops. I spy a couple from behind my lashes when a broad back shields my view of them.

And them from me...

The man is helping me. More folks pour into the elevator but he has me blocked from all angles, standing strong like a sentinel.

The elevator stops again and others empty out. Save for me and the man. I expect him to leave.

"What's your floor?" he asks, his voice sending warmth pooling in my belly.

"What?"

"I'm guessing you'd like to go change?" he speaks as if I'm reasoning too slowly. "On what floor is your room?"

"The sixth floor," I blurt, glad he's backing me and can't see my blushing face.

The elevator rides us back up and this time, no one else joins us.

"Thank you," my voice cuts into the silence.

He glances back, eyebrow lifted as if he has forgotten I'm here.

"For blocking me from their view."

He hums a sound I take as a 'you're welcome,' and goes back to watching the space ahead.

I'm mortified and I don't know why. Aside from his silence, this very handsome man doesn't mind helping me at all. And he hasn't once made me feel weird for being here and naked. Except for the initial look. What was that about?

The elevator's whirrs stop and the doors open. I start to step out but a hand grabs me by the elbow.

I turn to face him.

He shrugs off his jacket, giving me a front-row view of his bulging arms and firm pecs beneath his shirt.

I swallow. Loudly.

His eyes meet mine, a slight frown lining his forehead.

I clear my throat, gesturing around us. "The air's a bit... warm."

I have no scientific explanation for why that would result in an audible swallow and thankfully, he doesn't press for more.

He drapes his jacket around my shoulders and it falls to my mid-thigh. "It'll keep you covered on your walk down." He nods to the hallway. "I've got a meeting to attend."

"I... Thanks."

He nods and steps back into the elevator as the doors close.

Once I'm alone, I gasp, my eyes wide. What the fuck?!

I hurry to my room, let myself in, and shrug off the jacket. Shamelessly, I press it to my nose and—good lord, there's a hint of coconut and coffee and man. I take another whiff and fall back against the bed.

Something thumps. I sit up and search for the source of the sound. I find it next to a pillow. It's a wallet. His wallet.

Oh, no.

I flip it open and find a card with his name—Chance Easton. Other cards line the wallet but no money and no contact info.

I was going to find him and give him back his jacket anyway. So now, I've got to do it quickly.

"Fucking finally." Nat rolls her eyes as I walk into the Resort's lush gardens. "It's taken you years to get here. What happened?"

I give the colorful flowers a cursory glance before taking the seat next to her. "You won't believe what happened to me."

Nat squints. "Your eyes aren't red meaning it wasn't a whole lot of crying, so what?"

"Nat." I slap her shoulder. I cried only once with her about Todd's deceit. Now she wouldn't let up about it. "I wasn't crying. My dress tore."

"Where?" Nat checks me out.

"I changed out of that dress." Unfortunately, this one is equally sheer and fragile. "And a man helped me."

Nat's eyes are instantly twinkling. "You took a man to your room. You go, girl!"

"No, what?" My cheeks heat, because I thought exactly that—what if the brooding Chance Easton didn't have his meeting and followed me up to my room?

Before Nat's mind can run wild, I explain what happened.

"Oh, my." She fans herself with her hand when I'm done. "Knight in shining armor much. Where's the jacket and wallet? Let's find him."

"He said he had a meeting. I doubt he'd be at the hotel. I was thinking of handing them over to the receptionist."

"What? No way!" Nat grabs me by the shoulders. "Are you insane? You're going to hand them over to him yourself."

"I don't need to. Plus, I'm very embarrassed getting half-naked in front of him that way. I don't think I want to see him again." Even as I say so, I know that's a lie. I very much hope to see him again.

Nat reads me like her Thriller novels. "Yeah, right. You look like you want to see him again and I'm here to help you do just that."

"How?"

"Oh, you sweet summer child. I'm not telling you until the time is right."

The right time is late evening. The garden party has wrapped up and Nat and I head back to our floor.

"Be ready for dinner in fifteen. And look smoking!" she instructs and struts to her room.

"Dinner is at 7 p.m. It's only 5," I mutter to the empty hallway.

I enter my room and my gaze snags on the suit jacket. I grab it and resist sniffing. That's weird behavior.

I stall. No one will find out.

I press it to my nose and draw a deep breath. A shiver dances through me.

Quickly, I take a bath, put on a nice, casual evening gown, and tie my hair up. As ever, some ringlets fall loose and frame my face. Before I can stick them back up, there's a knock at the door.

It's Nat.

"Oh, my goodness!" she beams. "You look gorgeous, babe."

"You think?" A smile curves my lip. "I was thinking of just fitting these into..." I reach for the loose hairs but she swats my hands away.

"You look perfect. Don't touch anything."

"Okay." I take in her knee-length strapless dress and slick sandy blonde straight hair complete with expert-level makeup. "And so do you."

"I know." She flips her hair. "You're ready to go, right? Grab the jacket and wallet."

I do as I'm told and hurry to catch up as she's already out of the room. "Nat, but dinner is at seven. What are we doing?"

"Keeping a lookout for him."

I frown.

"Chance Easton? The man you want to bang?"

"Shut up," I say and she smiles.

We get into the elevator and I flashback to earlier today. I grab my dress, holding it close to my body. The elevator is empty, save for an older couple who pay us no attention.

"We are going to wait at the bar until he comes. If he doesn't, then..." She chews on her lip. "Well, he will have to come. He's staying here so why won't he?"

"Wait, do you expect me to run to him when he shows up and just accost him?" I'm gaping, because what?

Nat eyes me. "Um, not run, just walk elegantly." She nods at my heels with approval. "Did you want to hide in a corner and hope he finds you?"

I blow out a breath. "I guess not."

She throws an arm around my shoulder and pulls me to her side. "Look, it'll be alright. Just try to look less nervous."

That one would be a challenge.

We're at the bar for nearly an hour and Chance Easton is a no-show. I could distract myself with awing at the glistening bar top or the chandeliers hanging from the too-high ceiling or the many elegantly dressed folks gliding around looking rich, but no.

I'm nervous all over. Many scenarios run through my head. What if Chance isn't coming back? Would I go hours looking stupid carrying a suit jacket? What if he's looking for me elsewhere and thinks I made away with his card details?

"Another glass for my friend," Nat says to the bartender.

He proceeds to prepare another cocktail.

"She looks like she really needs one," Nat says to me.

"I don't."

"You do," she affirms. "Calm down."

"I can't. What if—"

"Shh." Nat presses a finger to my lips, her eyes glued somewhere behind me. "Tall, dark, and handsome in a white dress shirt and gray slacks?"

My heart palpitates. "Yes, sounds like him."

"Jesus, Mads. You should have invited him to your room."

"Nat, stop!" My stomach twists. "What is he doing?" I don't want to turn around and catch his eye.

"He's going to the receptionist. Wait, nope. He's coming over."

My eyes widen. "Here? What?"

"Not to us. Here to the bar."

Oh, God.

Inhale. Exhale. Panic.

I should have given over everything to the receptionist and never tried to meet him again. It wasn't like he hinted at anything earlier on. Hell, he only pitied me. I'd look more pitiful trying to get his attention again.

"He's seated. Now's your time to swoop in," Nat says.

I stay seated, my stomach quaking.

Nat does an exaggerated sigh. "Mads! Come on. Go!"

As she sees I'm not moving, an evil glint sneaks into her eye. She pulls me off the stool. I resist, but she manages to get me down.

"Go!" she whispers harshly, pushing me his way.

I stop, staring at his profile. His jaw is carved from marble, his frame strong and erect.

I inch forward, drawn to him. "Hi." He keeps looking at his phone, frowning. I clear my throat and try again. "Hi." I smile and wave.

He turns my way then. Deep blue eyes arrest mine.

I'm hooked.

Chapter Two

Chance

Owlish brown eyes make me lose my head for a few seconds. I see her lush pink lips moving again. She's speaking. To me. I don't hear a word, but I have to respond.

"How can I help you?"

Her eyes shutter.

Fuck. I must sound too brash.

"I came to give you these." She holds out my primly folded jacket. I didn't expect to get it back. "And your wallet. I found it in the jacket and thought you must have missed it. There was no money inside."

I collect the offering and place it on the counter. "I'm aware." I have no use for cash.

We stay that way for a few seconds. Long enough for me to register her lovely features I missed in the elevator because I was trying hard not to ogle her.

She's a brunette bombshell with arresting eyes and a cute oval face. She's not rail thin, but also not big either. Just somewhere in the middle that makes me want to pull her close and feel her softness.

I blink away those thoughts. Women aren't my thing. That's Baxter's thing, my little brother. I'm all work, no play.

Still, I'm sorely tempted by this brunette.

"Um, thanks for earlier, and have a goodnight." She starts to turn away.

"Sit. Have a drink." With me.

She spins, eyes curious. "Did you say something?"

I fucking did. What is wrong with me? I don't have time for this.

"Let's get a drink. Except, you're occupied." I glance behind her to the blonde whose eyes followed me from the moment I walked into the bar. I expected her to come over and then I would turn her down. That was my MO. I had no idea she was scouting for her friend.

The blonde looks away, whistling. I almost crack a smile. Almost.

The elevator train wreck turns back after looking at her friend too. "I'm not occupied."

"Good."

She climbs onto the barstool and fortunately for her, this dress doesn't split. That won't be easy to deal with in a place like this for sure. All eyes would be on her. But that door back there should lead to a private staircase to ensure she's well-hidden from sight.

"How was your meeting?"

My gaze falls on her. "Good."

No one cares what I do as long as it produces results. It's weird to be asked and I have nothing to follow that up with.

Silence lingers between us. She glances over her shoulder.

Despite not doing much talking, it's nice to have her next to me. If only to keep off the other ladies that try to get my attention.

"Want a drink?" I wave over the bartender before she decides she doesn't like sitting here after all.

"Yes, thank you." Her cheeks round with a smile, and my lips twitch.

Cute.

She orders a Malibu Sunset. The moment it comes, she's on it, pulling from the straw. It bubbles a sound—far louder than our non-existent conversation.

I set aside my feelings about, well, everything and order myself another Martini. "Your first time in Magic Island?" Her skin is still too fair, a clear sign she just showed up here.

"Yes. My bosses—well, former bosses granted me a weekend vacation to here." She gestures around. "It's amazing."

I nod. "Why former?"

She laughs, but there's hurt hidden behind it. "I was fired a week later. They clearly just wanted to do something to soften the blow. So they slot me in for this vacation and then I'm fired."

"That... must be hard."

"Nah." She waves a hand. "I'm having the time of my life here." She purses her lip. "Well, aside from that moment in the elevator. I'm not counting that."

I can't help the slight quirk of my lips.

She picks up on it. "You're laughing at me!"

"You have to admit, it was a bit hilarious."

"Not for me, it wasn't. I was mortified."

"And now?"

She presses slender fingers to her cheeks, blowing out a breath. "I am less so. Just don't tell anyone."

"Who would I tell?" I shrug.

"Well, for one. It'll make a good joke for your colleagues in your meetings." She sits up, face straight. "Guys, you won't believe this?" Her voice is a tad deeper. "This lady's dress got stuck in an elevator and she flashed me."

I frown. "Is that me? My voice?"

"Yeah, yeah. That's you telling my story and getting a kick out of it."

"I don't sound like that."

"Yeah, you do."

"And I don't talk that way."

"Ever heard yourself speak?"

"Every day."

"Like once or twice a day, because you don't speak much."

"No, just three times."

Her eyes glow with held-back laughter. "I could have sworn it was only two and a half times."

"Frankly, tops is two and three quarters."

She bursts into laughter, pressing her hand to her lips.

The sound is fresh and hearty and just what I need. The bar's getting busy. I want her all to myself.

"Want to take a walk?"

"Sure." She's off the barstool the next moment, but then her heel catches on the footrest.

She falls into me and I catch her easily. Her soft body melds into mine. I swallow a groan and in the same breath, get a whiff of her flowery fragrance. I want to pull her closer and smell her more but she pulls away, cheeks red.

"Um, sorry. I slipped."

"I saw." I nod to the bartender. He knows to put the drinks on my tab. "You okay?" I grab her elbow in a bid to steady her. But I leave my hand there because her skin is soft and smooth. I haven't felt anything this nice in a long time.

"Yes, I am."

I drift my hand to the curve of her lower back and guide her out of the hotel.

It's the biggest on the island, surrounded by gardens and backed by the ocean. Even from the entrance, the sound of the waves hitting the beach is discernible. It's a sight to behold at night, but for tonight, I want us to walk through the lit-up gardens.

The night sky is clear of clouds and spattered with stars and the air is cool and crisp.

"Wow." She pauses and tilts her head back. "Beautiful."

I'm arrested by her instead. The smooth curve of her neck and dip in her throat. Both slope down to the low neckline of her dress, exposing smooth skin and the top of her tits.

"Yes, beautiful," I rasp.

Her eyes meet mine and she smiles. Can she tell what I'm thinking?

If she can, she gives no indication. "Let's go."

"Of course."

I guide us toward the path, past benches with couples and a clear pool where a couple of folks are dipping. And then we break into the narrow trail. Lanterns with yellow lights line either side of the cobbled path.

"Oh, my. This is gorgeous!" she gushes, moving ahead of me. "I think I spotted this in the brochure. It's more beautiful than I imagined. You'd never find this in the city." She stops and squints into the copse of trees. "Are those fireflies?" she gasps. "There's a host of them. Have you ever seen so many?"

I don't get a word in. And I'm happy not to. Her awed excitement satisfies me. Takes my mind off the shit going on with me. I should be discussing with Baxter and Landon, my brothers. But here I am, trailing behind a brown-haired beauty whose name I haven't gotten yet.

She's a detour out of my strict schedule, just as she was in the afternoon. But like then, it's not unpleasant. Hell, it is very pleasant.

She halts. "Look! Another path." She points to the road that goes left. "Let's go there."

I haven't been down there before, but I'm certain it's safe whatever it is.

She doesn't wait for my reply and starts down the path. I follow her. We're surrounded by chirping crickets and buzzing insects and an even denser press of trees.

She's about to speak when her phone rings. She takes it out, eyes the screen. A frown instantly mars her lovely features. "I've got to take this."

She plunges ahead while speaking in harsh, short sentences.

My brows furrow as I stick close to her. I don't want to eavesdrop but it's quiet and I catch phrases like, 'stay away' and 'I want nothing to do with you.'

The call ends as we break into a space. A fountain bubbles in the center, surrounded by benches.

She sighs and sits on one of them.

I sit next to her and wait.

"It's my ex," she admits quietly. "We broke up two weeks ago because I caught him cheating. He wants to get back together," she scoffs, shaking her head. "Not in this life, we won't. But he won't stop trying."

"I'm sorry about that."

Her gaze whisks up to meet mine. "Sorry, I don't even know why I'm telling you. I just..." She blows out a breath, her shoulders sagging. "Nat thinks it's ridiculous the way I feel about it."

"And how do you feel?"

"Hurt." She chews on her plump lip. "I know we weren't on the best terms in the last year of our relationship but I was trying. I even considered therapy. Only to find out he was getting his fix with another woman."

She presses her eyes shut and turns her face up to the sky. The cool moonlight plays on her features, keeping me spellbound. "I want to do something. Just to take revenge on him and claim back some part of me."

"And that would be?"

Her eyes take on a curious light as she eyes me. "You're a stranger and I won't see you again after this weekend." Before I can speak, she presses on. "I can give you something I always felt uncomfortable doing with him."

"And what's that?" My voice manages to remain even, though my heart's thumping. Her voice has grown huskier and even though she hasn't said an explicit word, I already know where she's headed.

She kneels between my spread legs, a serene look in her gaze.

I do nothing, worried I'd spook her if I move.

She keeps her eyes on me and reaches for my belt buckle. Her fingers graze my length through my slacks. I close my hands into fists, watching her.

She tugs on the belt and loosens it. Then she goes for my zipper. Her eyes hold a question. I nod once and she continues, pulling down the zipper and exposing my briefs.

And my cock jutting against it.

A small gasp leaves parted lips. She exhales and palms me through the material.

An ache so sweet shoots from the spot through my veins. I grunt and thrust into the grip of her hand.

Her brown eyes are wide, her breath coming faster, her chest rising and falling. She drops her gaze to the point where she's touching me and strokes once, twice, and then licks her lips.

The need to claim her pink, chatty mouth overwhelms me, but I hold still. Going too hard now would scare her off. She has no idea who I am, or what I've put off because of my past. She's simply here to take what she needs and I have the instinct to give it to her.

She catches the waistband and tugs it low. My cock pops free, standing proud and tall. Cool air whispers on it, followed by the heat of her breath, and then she's closing her mouth around the head.

"Fuck me," I hush. My eyes go blind and I toss my head back.

Her mouth is soft and wet and hot, shooting pleasure like a drug straight into my brain. My ironclad control breaks and I spear my fingers into her hair.

I massage her scalp, encouraging and she rewards that with a moan that vibrates along my shaft.

I close my fingers around her hair and hold her still, then thrust upward twice, three times. She takes it like a champ, relaxing her throat so I can go deep.

"Fuck." I sink back against the bench, forcing myself to keep from deep-throating her until I finish. "Sure you don't like this?"

She pulls up from my cock, and her fist quickly replaces it, stroking. Her mouth glistens with her spit and my precum, and her chest is heaving, her tits nearly popping out. She's a sight.

"No. I don't." Her forehead scrunches. "Didn't. You taste..." She licks the slit at the tip of my cock and a groan tears from me. "Different." She does it again, oblivious to the agony she's putting me through. "Good different."

"Fuck," a growl tears from my throat. "Go back." I ease her head down. "Taste how good and different it is."

She moans at the back of her throat, her eyelids fluttering as she takes my cock in again. She squeezes the base as she sucks on the head and I'm in heaven. I throw my head back and heave at the night sky.

"Are you good?" she says from a cock-stuffed mouth.

I have to keep her talking. Need to see it.

I sit up and grab her chin, ensuring she stays on me. "Yeah, I'm good, but if I'm not, what would you do differently?"

"Probably take off my bra..." She chokes a little and shivers.

I sit forward, worried she's cold but no. Her eyes split and they're heavy with lust.

She's so turned on she's shaking, and I haven't even touched her yet. I'm going to and I'll make it more than good. But I need her talking.

I rub her cheek and feel my cock poking the inside of her mouth.

A deep rumble builds in my throat, my balls fisting. So fucking close.

"You'd take off your bra and...?"

It takes a few moments of slurping before her eyes focus. "I'll rub my tits all over your cock."

"That's a fucking sexy thought. Wanna show me those tits now?" I rasp.

She lets my cock go with a pop sound. The night chill replaces her warm mouth but it's no issue. In a second I'll be rewarded for my patience as she pulls at the sleeves of the dress.

"Maddie!" a voice calls out. "Mads!"

She goes still, her chest heaving, her wide eyes searching the dark around us. "That's Nat."

"You're Maddie?"

Nat calls again, her voice closer.

"Yes." She scrambles to her feet. With hurried motions, she picks up her purse. Her eyes are apologetic. "I've got to go."

I nod, ignoring my aching cock. I rise too and stuff it back. "You should. Your friend sounds worried."

Maddie backs away, her tongue sweeping over her lower lip nervously. It probably comes away with the taste of cock because she wipes her mouth with the back of her hands.

"Maddie!"

She gives me a look I can't decipher and heads off the way we came.

"I'm here!" her voice rings out moments later.

"Finally!" Nat is saying. "Where did you go? It's dinnertime."

I stand next to the fountain, disbelief leaving me cold.

I don't care that Maddie's trip here is only lasting a weekend. I must see her again and we'll finish what we started.

Chapter Three

Maddie

We have breakfast in the courtyard on Saturday. It's a warm morning but the air is cool. It whispers across my skin like a sweet kiss and I shut my eyes and absorb it. I draw a deep breath, enjoying the fragrance of flowers. It's everywhere at the resort.

When I woke up in the morning, I threw my window open only to be greeted by bird tweets and the sweet smell. The sun was a buttery circle in the sky, giving a sepia-like glow to everything below.

So unlike the city where car fumes and tall blocks of concrete were my good mornings. Ugh, and I have to go back on Monday.

Why couldn't this last forever?

"I don't see him anywhere," Nat murmurs.

I peel my eyes open and scan the courtyard. It's covered end to end in gazebos. Occupants of the hotel and surrounding villas chat over their breakfasts like us. But it's not noisy, just a gentle, soothing hum.

I should be focused on enjoying this but between dreading the trip back home and looking out for Chance, it's not a fun morning.

I sigh. "We can just stop. He's not coming."

"What do you mean?" Nat raises a brow. It's crazy how it looks so perfect when she only rolled out of bed thirty minutes ago. "We'll find him, trust me. And you're going to get some."

"No." I facepalm and she laughs. "That's not why I want to see him again."

Nat pulls my hand from my face so I can meet her eyes. There's humor dancing in them. "Look, I get it. You dated Todd for five years and you've grown into this..." She gestured toward me. "Prudish person. It's hard for you to come to terms with your wild side. But I'm very happy for you."

"Nat..."

"And I'm proud of you. I'm going to help you on your journey of becoming a wild sexy goddess that leaves a man trembling after you give him the best head he's ever gotten."

"Shh." I press my palm to her lips, fighting to suppress my laughter.

No one pays us any mind, but *still*.

Nat peels my hand off. "I'm sorry for last night. I just panicked. One moment I was sipping from the surprisingly delicious glass of Endless Summer and the next, you're gone. I mean, I'm all for getting the *D* but not at the cost of your safety."

"He'd never hurt me," I blurt without thinking.

Nat pauses, as I do. When did I grow such trust in Chance? It was only a night!

"I think," I add. Because she still watches me suspiciously, I change the subject. "I can't get over these tiny cakes."

Thankfully, she awes at the little treats with me. They're smaller than cupcakes, sweet and savory. I love them.

Once we're done with our breakfast, we hang around for a while. The gazebos empty out. With each person that exits, I'm sure Chance isn't coming.

"Let's go," I tell Natalie. There's no use hanging around anymore.

The sympathy in her eyes makes me feel a little guilty. I'm not mad at her. Just mad I missed the moment with Chance. It's not her fault I silenced my phone after Todd's call and didn't see her six missed calls.

"Cheer up." Nat squeezes my shoulder as we exit the courtyard. "We have that tour today, right? It's going to be mad fun and you can put Chance Easton out of your mind."

I don't tell her I'd rather keep the thoughts of Chance. They're like a breath of fresh air after being under water for too long.

Our tour guide, Stu, is assigned by the Resort. He's a local that knows the ins and outs of the Island. He drives us around pointing out the historical buildings and showing us the top spots to visit—a bustling market, a weekend carnival, and a spread of lush gardens.

That last one makes me blush for some reason.

We visit the Museum and spend half the time laughing over Nat's interpretation of the art. There's everything from paintings to marble sculptures to wooden artifacts. And... something made of metal and clay.

"Okay, now, that's freaky." Nat squints at the structure. "Fuck is that?" she asks Stu.

He gives her a good-natured smile. "It's the artist's demonstration of fertility. The joining of man's genius which is metal and the basic nature of the earth which is clay."

Nat and I share a look, then burst into laughter.

"It's brilliant," I say.

He only smiles in return. "Ready to see more?"

"Creepy fertility thingies."

"No more fertility thingies." He grins. "Just more of Magic Island."

"Cool, let's go," Nat chirps.

The tour guide drives past homes and buildings, then past greenery, then homes again. I'm awed.

I lean out the window, drinking the cool air tinged with a bit of saltiness from the ocean. I drop back into my seat and grin at Nat, feeling more alive than I've been in the longest time.

"I love this!"

She looks up from her phone. A small smile plays on her lips. "I can see that."

Smiling, I go back out and watch the passing terrain, tempted to leave my tongue hanging out like a dog.

"Magic Island is amazing!" I yell to no one.

"I'll show you amazing," Stu responds.

He stops beside the road. "We're here."

He gets out and we follow suit.

"There's only trees," Nat echoes my thoughts.

"Beyond them." He waves at us to follow and leads the way into the thick forest.

Nat and I eye each other. Feeling brave and excited, I head out. It takes a few minutes of walking before I hear Nat closing in behind me.

Her skepticism turns to awe as she beholds the sight before us. The sunlight dances through the covering of leaves and scatters in warm spots all over.

We both halt to take in the sheer magnificence of it.

"I think I died and went to heaven," Nat says.

Same.

"What are you doing?" Stu's voice shakes us out of our gaping.

"We're entranced by the amazing forest?" Nat throws her hands indicating the woods.

He laughs. "No, city girls. That's not amazing. This is."

We tread to where he stands. It's a few feet away. The closer we get, the louder the sound.

"What's that?" I ask, my curiosity piqued.

He stands immobile, aside from the growing smile on his face. When we come up next to him, I see it then. The whitest waterfall I've ever laid eyes on.

"Oh my," Nat breathes. "Truly amazing."

"That's not what's amazing," he says. "Come closer."

We draw nearer.

"Look." He points to the bottom of the waterfall where it meets the running river.

Right there, a myriad of colors flashes occasionally.

"What?!" I gasp. "How's that possible?"

"When the light hits the water just right, it creates such beautiful colors," he explains.

We say no more, content to soak in the beauty.

Nat comes out of her daze much quicker than I do and the clicks go off. "My co-workers are going to be jealous."

I don't have co-workers to brag to anymore. Or a lover to share this with. Just my parents. And this is not their kind of thing. Dad would ask if I caught fish and Mom would ask if I put on lotion to repel bugs.

Suddenly, a deep ache sits in my chest.

"It's beautiful. Can we go now?"

Nat and the tour guide don't argue.

I'm in a better mood the next day while Nat is the opposite.

"I think a bug got me." She rubs her neck and looks over the people having breakfast around us. "He's not here."

My worry for Nat overshadows my disappointment at not seeing Chance again. "Do we need to get some medicine for you?"

"Ugh, I don't like it. Is my head hot? I think my head is hot. My stomach hurts too. I'm tired."

It takes me five minutes of her whining to get why. "You're trying to get out of hiking!"

"I'm not." The corners of her lips twitch. "I'm ill."

"You're ridiculous, Nat. It's merely a walk."

"A long walk, a climb, and a host of other things. I don't want to destroy my ankles."

"And the heels you rock to work every day won't?"

She bites her lip.

"Look, it's going to be fun, okay?" She doesn't react. "I have a gift for you afterward."

She sits up and eyes me. "I hope you're not just saying so."

"Cross my heart." I do the mark. "You will get a present if you come on the hike."

"Can I complain about how stressful it is, though?"

"Nah."

She makes puppy eyes. "Please."

"Just for five minutes, that's all."

Nat grins. "That's all I need."

Dark brown hair catches my attention some gazebos away. My heart jerks. Could it be him?

The person starts to turn and I brace myself, holding my breath.

It's not him.

Disappointment sinks my shoulders.

I should have known. Chance fills a suit more than that and the cut of his jawline can be seen from miles away.

"What are you looking at?"

"Nothing." I drop my gaze.

The hike through the woods is exciting. We don't get to see another rainbow at the end of a waterfall. But get the view of mountains, running rivers and wildlife. Nat complains, but only a little. By the time it comes to an end, we're exhausted.

"I'm going to sleep for the next five years," Nat groans on our way up in the elevator.

"Just twenty-five. We have a massage appointment in thirty minutes."

"My surprise!" Nat squeals and squeezes me in a sweaty embrace.

After we clean up, we head to the spa. It smells of incense and I already feel relaxed, even before I lay on the massage table.

We watch the sun fall behind the ocean as we're lulled to drowsiness by the soothing massages.

The next morning, it's over. Our time on Magic Island has come to an end. I spend so long putting my clothes back in my suitcase Nat finishes and comes over to my room.

She takes one look at my face and a frown draws her lips down. "Maddie, are you sad we're leaving?" She draws me into a hug and squeezes. "Don't worry. We can do this again... Well, after we've saved for the next ten years, okay?"

I chuckle and pull away. Though I'm reluctant, I accept that good things come to an end.

I give the hotel a lingering glance as we ride down for the last time. It's bittersweet as we stop by the receptionist to hand our keycards over. I wish we didn't have to.

But the woman collects them and flashes us a smile. "Thanks for staying and we hope you come back soon sometime."

Probably never. "Thank you." I press out a smile.

"Miss Maddie?" a voice says behind us.

I half expect to see a hotel staff member offering to take our suitcases. But it's a man wearing dark sunglasses and a wire on his ear. Another man stands beside him with his hands folded. Both look very military.

I'm instantly worried.

"Y-yes?" I stutter. "May I help you?"

"Mr. Easton has requested your presence at once."

My heart lurches and my mouth dries up. I stare at him, unable to form words. Does he mean Chance?

Nat asks the question.

The man shifts his attention to her. "Yes, Chance."

"Why would he send you?" Nat drops the last word as if she tasted it and doesn't approve.

"I'm part of his security team." He turns back to me. "If you don't mind, can we leave now?"

I face Nat and I'm sure she sees the worry in my eyes.

"She's not going anywhere with you." She half-shields me with her body.

"You can come too."

"We have a flight to catch," Nat protests.

"And Mr. Easton wants to see you now." The man keeps his gaze on me. "What are you going to do, Miss Maddie?"

I look between Nat and the men and gulp.

Chapter Four

Chance

I pace my office. It was my father's before he retired and handed it over to me. I'd long replaced his art and photo frames of the family with nothing. Stripped down is my kind of style.

The only things I left were the shelves. They're stocked with old books about every subject known to man and every once in a while, I like to pick one up and learn something new while ignoring my real-life problems.

It doesn't work today. I can hardly see the words in the history text, my mind on what is to come. Or more rightly, who.

I glance at the door, expecting her to waltz in at any moment. Would she be mad? Happy? Indifferent?

I slam the book shut and fit it back on the shelf. My hands itch to fiddle with something so I spin the heavy watch on my wrist, over and over. When that proves unsatisfactory, I move on to the window and look out at the view. Ocean, trees, and buildings blended in perfect harmony.

Sometimes I watch the view until an idea sparks or a question is answered. Today, it gives nothing.

I look away, then pause. Am I... nervous? I press a palm on my chest. My heartbeat is a little quick, my palms are a little sweaty.

It can't be. I'm never nervous. I approach everything I do with precision and clear thought, almost knowing the outcome before it happens.

Yet, with her, I find myself unsure.

It's been two days since she raced out of the garden. The anxious look in her eyes just before she ran off prevented me from seeking her out.

I understand the thrill of one night of fun. Of having to forget. But when that's over, you want it done with.

I debated if that's what it meant to her and stuck with it. But I can only hold out for so long.

Today, I caved. Today, I decided to find her. It's her last day here, the last chance to finish what we started so I can get her out of my head.

My intercom buzzes. I know it's Ralph already. I don't wait for Julia to speak.

I hold down the button. "Send him in."

Ralph walks in.

I pocket my hands and plant my heels. Nothing would look more neurotic than me running across the room and grabbing him by the arms, shaking him, and asking him to tell me if she is here.

"Yes?" I raise an eyebrow.

"She's outside."

Fuck. My chest caves with relief. Inwardly, of course. Outside, I'm a statue, giving away nothing. "Send her in."

I hold my stance, watching the door. Waiting. And then finally, finally, I'm rewarded.

The door creaks open and she steps in. Maddie makes eye contact immediately and her sharp gaze nearly makes me back away. She's pissed.

Without taking her eyes off my face, she closes the door behind her and steps in, crossing her hands across her chest. "What do you want?"

Her words have a bite.

Good thing I'm prepared for her anger. "Have a seat." I gesture to the visitor's chair.

She eyes it and looks back at me. "Um, no? I have a plane to catch. I don't have time to sit and chat."

The purse of her lips juggles my memory. It looks just as it did when she had her mouth around my cock in the garden—full and red and delicious.

Her gaze shifts with my silence.

"We'll stand and speak, then." I step forward. "Maddie, it's nice to meet you again."

She says nothing.

"I hope Ralph wasn't rough with you. I instructed him to be careful."

"I'm fine." Her eyes sweep up and down my frame and her anger drops a notch, replaced by another look I recognize. "Why am I here?"

"I have a proposal."

Her eyes narrow.

"A job proposal." I pick up the brown folder and hand it to her.

She collects it reluctantly. "I didn't ask you for a job."

"But I remember our conversation. You don't have a job back home. And my assistant quit just recently. It will take at least three weeks to find someone suitable. I'm hoping you'd be willing to do the job till then."

A frown pulls her brows together. "And this is?" She waves the folder.

"All the terms of the agreement if you're to take this job."

Throwing me a skeptical look, she flips open the folder. I watch her face, anticipating her reaction when she gets to the bottom of the page and sees the figure.

She doesn't disappoint.

She gapes and looks at me with rounded eyes. "For three weeks?!"

I nod.

"Sure you didn't add a zero by mistake?"

"I'm positive," I respond.

She presses her mouth shut and closes the folder. Her skepticism is back. "Did you offer so much money just so I can't refuse?"

"Can you be bought?" I challenge.

"No."

"I didn't think so. That's the true pay."

She opens her mouth and shuts it, then looks away from me.

I see the debate in her eyes, the back and forth with herself. I can't tell which part of her is winning but my fingers are crossed for the one that keeps her here on Magic Island.

"I don't have a place to stay," she murmurs.

"You'll be given a suitable accommodation."

She eyes me.

"Not with me." A chuckle threatens to fall from my lips, but I swallow it. "It's still at the Resort but superior to where you stayed earlier."

"Oh…" She eyes me. "A job that pays three times my former salary in three weeks, a place to live on the coveted Magic Island and what else?"

"What else?"

"The catch. There must be. What do you want from me?"

I glance at her lips. "Nothing."

"Huh." She chews on her lower lip as if to torture me.

I look away and focus on my mahogany desk. The need to pounce on her, pull that lip from her teeth, and ravish it is too strong.

Something happened in the last two days and she's grown immune to me. I just have to remind her what we shared, but not here or now.

"I will take it."

My head whips up. "You will?"

She nods. "I have nothing to go back to." She shrugs. "This might be a nice change of pace for me and by the way, I love Magic Island. An extended stay here won't be bad."

I don't smile in triumph as I want to. I only nod. "Good. We'll both be getting what we need."

"Hold on." She hurries over and stands opposite me. Only the expanse of the desk keeps us apart. "You didn't ask for my résumé. I've never worked as a PA before."

"That's no problem. It's intuitive and Julia would be happy to help."

"Julia?"

"The secretary."

"Oh." She chews on her lip again.

My cock twitches. She needs to do that less if I'm to get any work done with her around. Or maybe I should stop looking at my new assistant too much.

The door opens. I already know who it is before he walks in. Only one person enters my office like it's their living room.

"Chance." Baxter splays his arms like we're buddies and it's been too long since we saw each other. We met in a meeting an hour ago. His grin is broad and a smile crinkles his eyes. "What are you—" His eyes fall on Maddie and I swear to god, they take on that hazy look that every woman falls for. "Hello, there."

He advances, somehow managing to look broader than he already is. He's like me. We value gym time and have built ourselves into looking like we model for a living.

Where I cover mine up with suits to look professional, Baxter is the opposite. Vain as they come, he wears a shirt a size too small that hugs his frame. He leaves the first two buttons open, exposing a peek of chest hair that he claims is a lady magnet.

It's unprofessional. Everything about him from his messy styled hair to his tight black pants and too-friendly personality. But because he's my brother, I'm forced to work alongside him for the good of everyone.

"Don't *hello there* her." I glare at Baxter. "Do you need something?"

"Nothing from you, old man." He focuses his full attention on Maddie. "Tell me he dragged you in here so I can rescue you."

She smiles. "I wasn't dragged."

"Oh?" He leans in close to her and whispers, "That's his style."

"What a style!" She puts on a disbelieving look and shakes her head.

"You know, right?" Baxter backs up and does the *what the hell* expression. "I just have to tame him sometimes. Without me, he'll be a feral beast."

Maddie throws a glance in my direction and laughs. "Really?"

Baxter nods, serious. "When we were young, our dad used to say, 'Watch your older brother, Bax. He's dangerous, even to himself.'"

"No one has ever said that."

My protests go unheard as Maddie laughs at Baxter's antics.

My neck prickles with irritation. How can she find him funny?

She laughs so much she places a hand on his arm for support and I nearly lose it. She wouldn't even crack a smile at me today and now she's laughing and touching Baxter.

"Bax, you can get out." My voice is hard steel. "You have no business here."

Maddie's laughter cuts off and she looks away.

Shit. Even though it wasn't directed at me, I loved the sound. Still, I'm not willing to entertain any more of Baxter if he's taking all her attention.

"Come on, man. We're just ribbing. Don't kill the fun." He glances sideways. "Look how you've made... What's your name?"

She blinks up at him. "Maddie."

"Maddie...?" His smile is charming.

"Maddie Lowe."

Look at that. She's giving him her last name.

"Well, I'm Baxter Easton. The hottest of the Easton brothers." He stretches a hand.

"Nice to meet you." She slips her hand into his.

He smiles broadly and she smiles back.

"Lovely smile," he says.

"Baxter," I say through clenched teeth. "Get. Out."

"Can I take Miss Lowe with me?"

"Not in your life. Never."

"Whoa... So defensive." He still holds her hand. "I'm getting the impression"—he glances at the folder on the desk—"that Miss Lowe has been offered a job here. Shouldn't I get to know the woman I'd be working alongside?"

"No need for that. You're not going to see her."

"I see her now though." He looks down at her. "And I like what I see."

I look away to avoid Maddie's inevitable blush. He always makes the ladies blush. He relies heavily on his charms and convinces every woman within his immediate vicinity to swoon at him. Every woman is fair game, except taken women—girlfriends and wives.

Girlfriends and wives.

My mind churns.

My gaze shoots up, going between Maddie and Baxter. They aren't touching anymore, but he still has her spellbound. What they're talking about, I have no idea.

I cut in anyway. "Maddie is my girlfriend."

"Excuse me?" Maddie says at the same time Baxter's brows shoot up.

"Oh? I had no idea you were seeing someone."

Maddie starts to speak.

"Maddie. Honey."

Her gaze whips to my face, confusion playing across her features.

"Let's not argue in front of Baxter, okay? I knew you wanted to keep it private for a while, but what's the harm? He's my brother." I sound patronizing, unlike myself. But it's working. She's realizing she needs to play along.

"Alright, babe." She blesses me with a big smile.

So this is what Baxter was enjoying just moments ago?

I look back at him. "So, what do you want? Nothing? Great. Leave."

"No, no, no." Baxter's frown morphs into a grin.

I hate what's coming already.

"How do you get a girlfriend and not let everyone know? Bring her to dinner this Sunday so she meets the family."

There's alarm written on Maddie's face. Even I feel my stomach clench.

"No."

"No?" He lifts a challenging eyebrow. "If you don't bring her, then she's not your girlfriend and you're a scared little—"

"Fine," I bite out. "We're coming to dinner."

Baxter grins. "I look forward to seeing you. Miss Lowe." He tips his head and heads out with a jaunty step after he's just caused so much damage.

The punk.

Chapter Five

Maddie

I leave Chance's office in a daze. Nat is still where I left her in the waiting room. She rushes over and clasps firm hands on my shoulders. "What happened? Are you okay?"

I gulp and nod.

She calms down. "Good." Her eyes roam over me. "What did he say to you?"

I'm still with the folder, so I hand it over.

She takes it while eyeing me. "What's this?" Without waiting for my reply, she flips it open. She gasps. "What the hell?"

I pull her to the edge of the room so we're out of earshot of the secretary. Julia, I think.

"Is this for real?" She stares at me with wide eyes.

"Yep."

"Damn!" She looks at the agreement again, her eyes locked on the salary, and then back up at me. "What did you say to him? I mean, it's a lot of money for three weeks but you have your life to return to."

I bite my lips and her face falls.

"You accepted?!" She gapes. "Maddie!"

"Nat, please hear me out." I grab her arm and squeeze. "I love it here and this is a great opportunity for me. It's out of my comfort zone and a little daunting, but nothing good in life isn't."

"Well..." She eyes me. "Where will you stay? You certainly can't afford our vacation rooms."

"He promised to provide accommodation."

She blinks rapidly, probably thinking of another argument.

Before she can voice it though, I look at her with pleading eyes. "Can you support me on this, please?"

She heaves out a breath. "Mads... you know I'll support you on this. But I'm a bit selfish too. I'll miss my new roommate."

I moved to Nat's after the breakup with Todd. It was a fun two weeks indeed. I'll miss her too.

I draw her into a hug. "It's only three weeks."

"Not a day more." She squeezes the air from my lungs.

I yelp, laughing. "I promise."

She pulls back and cups my face. "I trust you'll do a great job, Mads. And while you're working so closely with him, make sure you get that D."

I glance back at the secretary. She pays us no attention. I smile, rolling my eyes. "Yes, ma'am."

It's only an hour left before the plane takes off. I insist on accompanying Nat to the airport. We're leaving when Chance's men come up to us.

"Mr. Easton asked us to take you."

Nat and I exchange a look and shrug.

They zoom through the traffic and make it in time. I stay and watch Nat go through to the terminal, my heart jumps. Will I be able to enjoy Magic Island all by myself? Nat's presence made it special.

I'm still musing on that when she spins around, dancing while pointing at her ticket and pointing up.

I'm confused. "What?" My voice hardly carries in the noisy airport.

She's still doing it, grinning like it's her birthday.

"What?!" Is she just excited to fly? I'm confused—*what's going on?*

"Mr. Easton upgraded her ticket to first class," a voice supplies over my shoulder.

"Oh." Why would he do that? A queasy feeling starts in my stomach. I push it away and wave at Nat with a big smile.

She blows kisses back at me and then disappears through the door.

I drop my hand and blow out a breath.

I'm alone.

With only a few strokes of the pen, I've sealed my fate in Magic Island for the next three weeks. Only time will tell if I've made the right decision.

"Can we leave now?" Ralph says.

"Sure." I follow them out of the airport.

Despite the foot we started on today, the men are okay. Mostly silent but still proactive and Chance trusts them, so I don't care to ask where we're going.

They bring me back to the Resort.

I sit up, ready to get out, but they drive straight past the hotel and deeper into the expansive grounds of the Resort.

Curious, I lean against the window and watch the villas we drive past. They are wooden structures with finely carved porch railings. In between them are paths for walking, then flowers and trees.

The car stops.

"We're here," Ralph announces.

I get out and look up at the villa in front of us. "Here?"

"Yes," he answers. He comes round the car and takes my suitcase out of the trunk. Then he leads the way up the porch steps to the door.

He waits until I'm next to him to hand me a key. "This will be your home while you're here."

"This? Are you sure?"

His dark glasses cover his eyes but I can tell he's looking at me like I'm being ridiculous.

I shut my gaping mouth and insert the key. If a look through the Resort's website didn't prepare me for the luxury of the villas, I'd have passed out seeing this for the first time. Even so, I'm so awed I don't walk in. Just stand at the door and worry that this is too much.

Nat and I flipped through the images and guffawed at the thought that my job would give us a villa to stay in. Now, look at me. For a job I haven't even started, my new boss is assigning me a luxury apartment.

What?

"Is it... to your liking?" Ralph asks.

My head whips sideways. "Yes, it is. Very much so," I chuckle.

He doesn't share my joke. "Good. If you need anything, there are numbers on the phone to call the Resort staff. Enjoy your stay, Miss Maddie."

He turns and leaves.

I'm still standing there when the car drives off. Eventually, I pull myself out of my daze and wheel my suitcase in.

I shut the front door behind me and take a tour.

Everything is wooden. From the high, beamed ceilings to the floor underfoot. The lamp on the table is wooden and the art on the wall is carved from wood. All in different shades that blend so nicely.

The only things not in the warm brown are the plants. Green, bright, and fresh, I start to wonder if they're fake. I touch a leaf and it darkens. Wow.

I move on to the kitchen and marvel at the still brown countertop but polished marble. I open a cabinet, shocked to find it stocked with cereal. I flip open all of them. There's food for weeks here.

Excited, I check out the bedroom. There's a queen-sized bed next to the window. I slide onto it, sighing at the bouncy, soft feel of it. Outside my window, there are trees and a garden of flowers. The air smells like it too. And though I can't see the ocean, the salty tang is in the air.

I shut my eyes and roll around in bed.

I'm guessing I'd like working for Mr. Easton a lot.

I'm at work early the next day. Julia smiles as I walk in her direction.

"Maddie! It's lovely to see you."

I'm taken aback. She didn't pay me much mind the previous day. But it's hard not to return her smile. She seems to radiate joy.

"Julia, right?"

"Yes." She stands and offers her hand.

I can't help but compare our outfits. Back at home, I have a closet full of skirts and pantsuits. My work required it, and I always looked sharp in them.

Here, I'm unsure what the standard dress code is. And even if I do know, I'm not sure how to get it.

Julia is in a cream blouse and a skirt that cuts off just below her knees. Her golden blonde hair is done up in a bun and she's light on the makeup.

I think I'm okay in my short-sleeved blouse and straight pants. These are the only outfits I have that look remotely professional. I won't worry about that now though. Best to get through my day one first.

"You're welcome." She starts to rifle through the files on her desk. "So, this is for you." She hands me a bulky file. "And this too."

I collect the laptop and balance it on the file. "What are these?"

"They contain everything you need to know about Mr. Easton's schedule. His meetings, appointments, and travel plans. They're all in there." She looks up at me. "He's usually in the office at eight-thirty. Earlier on some days, but I'm guessing you have…" she glances at her watch. "Fifteen minutes to know what he's going to do today. You can work on the rest when you're not too busy. Any questions?"

I blink. "No."

Julia's face softens. "I know this a lot. But it's not so bad working with Mr. Easton. At least you don't have to deal with everyone else on the floor bugging you about everything."

I smile at her eye roll. "Thank you, Julia." I look around. "Where can I set up?"

"Two doors down the left hallway. There's a conference room that's rarely in use."

"Thank you."

"Hey," her voice stops me as I start to walk away. "Call me if you need anything."

I smile gratefully and leave for the conference room.

I set my phone's timer for fifteen minutes and get to work. Chance's data is well-organized. Thank goodness for the past PA. They did a good job of keeping his schedule clean.

I run through what he has to do today. Meeting, meeting, a few errands—which I'm sure I'd be running, and another meeting. He'll be done by six p.m.

Wow.

When I'm done reading that, I flip through the file to understand the subject of the meetings and the people involved.

The timer beeps and I pack up, certain I'm ready.

"He's in," Julia says as I walk past.

I stop by the door and exhale before giving a quick knock and then turning the door handle.

Chance sits behind the desk, his eyes glued to his laptop screen. A line is between his brows, his lips tight.

I venture forward. "Good morning."

He glances up and his expression clears in an instant.

I smile, hoping he'd return it, but he doesn't. I let the smile drop.

"Need something?" he asks.

"No. I'm just here to inform you that your first meeting for the day is at nine a.m. And ask if there's anything you'd like me to do?"

He sits back, brows furrowed. "You've gone through the schedule and everything?"

"Not everything." I smile down at my heels but look up with a straight face. His surprise is thrilling. "Just today's tasks."

"Good." He looks thoughtfully at his laptop, before meeting my eyes again. "There's nothing for you to do right now, just go prepare for the meeting. You'll be attending it too."

I smile. "Great, I'll go do that." I turn to leave.

"Maddie?"

I do a one-eighty. "Yes?"

"It's impressive you showed up early and got ready."

"Thank you," I say and leave.

That's the last time he compliments my work. The rest of the day is all business. Meeting to meeting and running errands, which I don't mind given that Ralph drives me around.

By the time I get home, I'm a zombie.

I manage a quick meal and drop into bed and I'm out.

I wake up to sunshine and a cool breeze on my face. I start to smile when my brain kicks into action.

I have to get to work!

After a quick shower, I pace before the closet. None of my clothes look made for the business environment at the office. What am I going to do?

I eye the clock. I set an early time for myself yesterday. I can't fail.

I grab a short black skirt. It has frills but it's better than the bright orange one and the white one that stops under my butt. This one reaches a few inches above my knees. I pick a crop top that sits just above the waistband of the skirt. And that's the best I can do. I refuse to look at myself and slip on my shoes, grab my purse and the laptop, and head out.

I'm walking through the quiet lanes in between the villas when my senses prickle. I pause and look around. There's no one out here. Why does it feel like there's someone, though? I shake off the thought and keep walking.

By the time I get a cab, I'm many minutes too late.

We turn a corner when a flash of black catches my peripheral view. A car trundles many paces behind us. When we take another road, it's still there.

My stomach coils. This doesn't feel right.

"Hey, can you take another route?" I ask the cab driver.

"It'll cost you more money."

"I'll pay. Just go."

He changes lanes and crosses into another street. Thankfully, the black car no longer trails us.

I hope I haven't taken too long but when I get to the office, the nine a.m. meeting is underway. Slowly, I crack open the conference room door. Faces turn toward me. I ignore them and keep my gaze on *him*.

He's not smiling. At all.

I've fucked up.

Chapter Six

Chance

I'm listening to my employees debate when she walks in. Silence descends over the meeting. Everyone's looking at her and my blood starts to boil.

She shouldn't be coming in with that outfit—a flirty black skirt and a white top that shows off creamy skin. She looks like a meal and the staff, both men and women, stare at her like they want a piece.

"Ramsey," my voice has their gazes swinging back to me. "Please, go on."

He clears his throat and resumes speaking.

While decorum is restored to them, my eyes wander. She's coming around the long conference table, her gaze glued on me. I hold it, giving away nothing. Her brown eyes dim. She probably thinks I'm mad. Should I be?

I'm the opposite though. Just the sight of her fills me up with an energy that pumps through my body, and goes straight to my cock.

Especially given how she looks this morning.

The spot by my left is empty for her and she drops her file and laptop, then comes over to whisper in my ear. I get a whiff of her sweet scent and a peek of cleavage and I'm done for.

She says something about being late, but I can't respond. My throat is tight. The only thing I want to do right now is take her. Away from this meeting, away from this building, to my home. I want her lying beneath me as I take off all her clothes.

She pulls away and sits down, her eyes down.

Now, I'm mad. With barely any effort, she makes me feel things I shouldn't. She makes me want things I can't have.

I curl my fingers around a pen and squeeze. It's me who offered her a reason to stay. If I didn't she'd be long gone and I wouldn't be in this fix.

It's my fault. And I'm going to fix it the only way I know how.

My gaze slashes to the left and I catch her watching me. She doesn't look away.

"Mr. Easton?" Ramsey's voice pulls me back into the meeting.

He's the head of the marketing department and so far, he hasn't been able to show me a feasible marketing strategy for the next few months.

"Yes, Ramsey? Do you have something new for me? All I've gotten for the past week are rehashed unsuccessful attempts that did nothing but waste the company's resources."

"I understand, sir." Ramsey sits up and pulls at his collar.

It's cold in here from the AC.

"B-but I have something good. Something better."

"And that is?"

"What if we don't attack the campaign with ads but we do a giveaway that will attract more patronage?" He holds his breath, waiting.

"I'm listening."

"We select a few products and put them out in an advert that drums up the public's interest. Once they can test the authenticity of these products, they will come back for more."

"Freebies don't work."

I pause. Did she just speak? I turn in Maddie's direction. Everyone is looking at her as I am.

"Sorry." She presses a hand to her lips. "That just came out."

"No, no." I face her. "I want to hear more. What are your thoughts on Ramsey's proposal?"

She looks around the table but focuses on me. "Freebies don't work," she reiterates. "My former boss tried it and it was a nightmare. You don't want to cater to people who don't have purchasing power for your product at full price."

"So? That's the point!" Ramsey says. "They'll tell the people they know who will buy."

"It doesn't work like that. A friend to a person who can't purchase, most likely can't purchase too. It's just—"

"What do you know?" Ramsey snaps. "You're just a mere—"

"Ramsey," I cut in before he tempts me to fire him. "This is a civil discussion."

"But she's not even from my department!" He's red in the face. "How does she dare to advise me? I've been doing this for years!"

"And clearly, you've run out of fresh ideas. Instead of defending the old ways that don't work, maybe it's time to find something new."

He sits back, chastised but I don't miss the annoyed look he throws Maddie's way.

It's harmless. His pride is hurt, that's all.

I meet her eyes to ensure she's all right. She's looking at me, a soft look in her brown gaze.

Uncertain what that's about, I move the meeting from marketing to another department. The meeting ends an hour later.

I make my way into my office. I'm supporting a semi and I need to get rid of it now, as well as the thoughts of Maddie tumbling through my head.

How she chewed on the bottom of a pen. How her slender fingers moved over the keyboard. How she tucked her lip between her teeth when typing very fast.

I want her and I can't wait.

I press the intercom. "Send Maddie in," I tell Julia.

"Straightaway, sir," Julia replies.

Not two minutes later, Maddie walks in. She stops halfway across the room, her gaze lowered. "You called for me?"

"Yes." I'm sitting behind my desk. I'd rather be standing next to her. But the semi has gone full steel again. "Have a seat."

She takes the spot opposite me.

Before I can speak, she blurts, "Sorry that I came in late and I interrupted the meeting. I will make sure to avoid doing both again."

"That's not why I called you in here."

Her gaze whisks up. "Oh. Why, then? I was sure I was getting a slap on the wrist."

My lips twitch. "No." I sit up, fighting the urge to adjust. "I can see you're having some trouble."

"Trouble?"

"Yes, finding something suitable to wear."

Her cheeks turn red. "Excuse me?"

"You don't think a barely there dress is office wear, do you?" She gapes. Before she can say more, I slide my card across the desk. "Take this as a clothing allowance and get something suitable to wear."

She eyes the card and looks at me. "I don't appreciate you talking about my clothes."

I shrug. "You're my assistant. You must appear in a way that doesn't distract everyone at the office."

She looks at me through her lashes. "Distract everyone?"

I swallow. "Yes, everyone."

A mischievous glint sneaks into her eyes. "I don't think there's anything wrong with my clothes."

"Really?"

"Mm-hm. Do you want to tell me what's wrong with it?"

Everything that's wrong with it flashes through my head. "I can't say," my voice comes out hoarsely.

"Sure, you can," she taunts and rises.

The desk is covering most of her lower body but a bit of her creamy thighs are visible.

"Maddie," I murmur.

She spins around giving me a flash of her supple ass cheeks when the bottom of her skirt flies up.

I bite back a groan.

"Is this bad?"

"Come this way, Maddie," I rasp. "Come see how bad it is."

Maddie's eyes orb and she comes around the desk. I lean back in my seat and swivel so I'm facing sideways. She stops before me, her eyes falling down my gently heaving chest to the tent in my slacks.

Her eyes turn heavy-lidded. She runs her tongue over her bottom lip and I groan. She's probably thinking of the moments in the garden. I am too.

But we aren't in some garden hidden away in an exotic resort. We are in the middle of the business district. Floors up. The muted sounds of the busy office coming in.

But for all I care, we could be alone in the world.

"Do you see, Maddie? That's what skirts like that do."

"Oh," she says. "You can't go around like this?"

"No." I palm my length through my slacks and stroke, up to down.

Maddie's eyes follow my movements, growing hungrier by the second. She licks her lip again and it comes away wet.

I want it wet with my precum. Just like that night.

"Maddie."

"Yeah?"

"Remember how you got down on your knees? So eager, sucking my cock off like it could quench your thirst?"

She drifts closer until she stands between my legs.

"You wanna finish what you started? Hmm? My cock has missed your eager mouth."

She goes down then, crouches before me. Her hands are quick to displace mine. She tugs on my belt and zips me down. Seconds later, my cock is sticking out of my slacks.

Thick and veiny.

She sucks in a breath before diving in. It's as I remembered. No, better.

I shut my eyes as sensation pours through me. Her mouth is wet and warm, rivaling the chilly AC. While her hand works the base, her tongue rolls around the head.

She flicks the slit with the tip of her tongue and I see stars.

I grab her hair, unsure whether to push her down and get more and pull her back because it's too much.

Her moans get louder as I direct her movements, showing her how deep to go and when to let up.

She's so hungry for it that when my grip slackens, she takes me into her throat.

Fuck! I tear my eyes open to see it for real, to believe that she's doing this.

She's looking at me. Her mouth at the base of my cock, her nostrils flared to receive more air.

The sight of her threatens to make me cum. I jerk back and she lets go, pulling in a gasping breath.

"That's enough." I pull her to her feet. "Show me what's hiding under your lacy underwear."

I draw her close until her hips are level with my face. Breathing raggedly, I yank up her skirt. "Hold."

She does as she's told.

I spend a second marveling at the spread of her underwear on her pussy lips, then I slide it to the side. I push a finger in to find that she's wet and ready.

She moans, her knees beginning to tremble.

I ease her closer and she gets my intention quickly. She straddles my thighs, her knees on either side.

Grabbing her hips, I lower her down. My cock pokes her, searching for an entrance. It dawns that her underwear is still on.

It's a flimsy piece of cloth and it takes only a twist of my fingers to take off. I pocket it and proceed to slide her down.

"Wait!" Her haze is gone, replaced by panic. "I'm on the pill and I got tested recently, I'm clean but—"

"I'm clean too."

She believes me instantly, her gaze growing heavy. "Fuck me then."

A lump forms in my throat. To stamp out that sensation, I plunge into her. She closes around me like a glove to a fist. It's so good I throw my head back on a groan.

She falls forward, her face in the crook of my neck. She grips my shoulders, trembling. Her hips circle and I see stars.

I want more.

I capture her hips and help her ride me harder, better.

She's moaning. Her screams combined with my groans fill the office. We're loud, but that's alright. No one comes into my office unannounced—except Baxter and he's away. No sound leaves because it's insulated that way.

It's just us two.

I bounce her so she's louder, proving just how good she's getting it.

"I'm so close," she whimpers.

I wrap my arms around her to keep her steady and then I'm thrusting upward, grinding against her clit.

"Fuck. Oh, fuck! Chance."

She starts to tremble, her legs shaking.

My orgasm hits me seconds later. I groan to the ceiling, holding her hips still so I can shoot every drop of my seed into her. She takes it with enthusiasm, bouncing on my lap. Then her pussy spasms, pulling out the last drops of cum.

Finally, she collapses on my chest.

I hold her still and rub a hand up and down her back as we both catch our breaths.

The intercom beeps and I lean forward to press it. Maddie moans as I move inside her. I bury her face against my chest for her to muffle her sounds.

"Yes?"

"Sir, the CFO is here to see you. Should I let him in?"

Maddie starts to scramble off me, but I hold her steady with a firm grip. "No. Tell him to wait."

I let go of the button and face Maddie. Her hair is a mess, and her eyes still look hazy. Maybe because we're still joined. I rock a little and she whimpers.

"The CFO..."

"Yeah." I let her go grudgingly.

She slides off me and rights her clothes, then brushes her hair with shaky fingers.

Without saying a word, she turns to leave.

"The card."

She spins and picks it up, then walks out on shaky legs.

Chapter Seven

Maddie

I stop by Julia's desk as I'm about to leave the office.

She turns up her face with a smile. "How was your second day? Anything interesting happen?"

Did she hear me and Chance? I search her face. She's only asking to be friendly, right?

"No, no. Just the usual." I shrug.

Her eyes narrow.

Before she can prod some more, I ask, "Hey, do you know where I can find work appropriate outfits?" I gesture at my outfit. "The boss thinks this isn't it."

Julia presses out a sympathetic smile. "I didn't want to tell you, but yeah, this is extremely cute but it has everyone talking."

"Ugh." I slap my forehead. "I'm ready to get something else. So, where do I go?"

"You know what?" Julia stands. "I'm done with work. How about we go together?"

"Great, let's."

We take a cab to a busy street and Julia alights in front of a store.

"What's your budget?" she asks as we walk in.

"I don't know. I'm guessing things are priced differently here than in the city."

"Very different." She walks down an aisle. "We just need to know the price range we can go for. This is where I shop. It has high end, low end, and middle end." She chuckled. "You get my meaning."

"Whatever is fine, I guess. Chance gave me his card and didn't really put a spending limit on it."

Julia halts and spins around. Her eyes are orbs and I back up a bit. She follows me step for step until she grabs me by the shoulder. "What did you say?"

"Chance gave me his card?"

"Yes, and no spending limit?!" She gapes.

"Yes, he didn't s—"

She takes my hand and races us out of the store. How she's able to manage that in heels is a mystery to me.

"Julia? Where are we going?"

"You mean you can buy anything? Then we are going to the biggest, bestest store!"

She pulls me into another building with a doorman and a staff rushing to welcome us.

"I'll take a glass of champagne, please," Julia says with a flourish.

I say nothing and she shoulders me.

"Same," I murmur.

While that staff is occupied with bringing us the wine, another comes over and asks what we need. We are shown to a sitting area while a rack of outfits are wheeled to us.

Julia sips on her wine, nodding to selections or saying nah.

"More wine." She holds out her empty glass.

"Julia!" I elbow her side.

She laughs. "Girl, this is the dream. You better live it."

I follow suit and relax, pretending I can actually afford this kind of service.

We move on to testing the clothes and they all feel decadent on my skin, fitting my frame perfectly.

"I'm not sure what to go with!" I tell Julia when I'm done.

"Why do we have to choose?" She winks. "You have the magic card."

Jesus. "You're wild."

She giggles and asks the staff to bag all of them.

I have a mini heart attack when I see the bill. I grip the card tight, sure it's illegal to spend this much money on mere clothes.

Julia snatches it from me and hands it over to the cashier.

Once that's over, we arm ourselves with two bags in each hand and step out into the clear night.

"Now we need to get you bags and shoes." Julia races along, looking into the next store.

"Julia…" I warn. "Haven't we spent too much already?"

She spins to me. "What?" There's a frown scrunching up her nose. "What are you talking about too much?"

"Well, just because he didn't put a spending limit doesn't mean I should empty the account."

She laughs like I've told a joke. "Maddie, please. You're so precious." She draws close. "Look, even if you tried, you wouldn't get to the last dollar of Chance Easton's account."

I frown. "What does that mean?"

"That he's rich, rich." She throws a cursory glance around us. "Billionaire rich, and that's just him. His brothers, his family, they own all of this." She waved her hands around us.

My stomach knots. "The street?"

"The whole Island and half of the businesses here. The rest pay a hefty fee to them to operate."

"Wow."

"Yeah." She nods. "So saying you can't buy some shoes and bags, that's like an insult to him. If he gave you his card, he means you should do with it as you please."

I'm unable to breathe. When I learned Chance is the CEO of his company, I assumed it was just that small world he controlled. Not the entire fucking world I now live in.

"You okay?" She tilts her head to the side.

"Yes." I nod quickly.

Oh, god. I fucked him. I went down on him and rode his cock and now... I'm just a city girl. Nothing to my name. And he's... he's... practically a god here.

"Come on." Julia pulls me along and into another store.

I don't feel less guilty spending more of his money just because he's rich. But Julia is a force and I go along with it.

Low-key, getting nice things feels nice.

By the time we're done, I'm smiling for no reason. Maybe because of the too many wines the stores provided us automatically.

We stand on the sidewalk, done for the night.

"Thank you so much, Jules."

"Hey, you called me Jules." She pokes my cheek. "My mom calls me that."

We giggle and she hugs me.

"Thanks for inviting me along, Maddie. It's nice to have a glimpse of what it means to be Mr. Easton's special girl."

The alcohol haze drops a notch. "What?"

"Everyone at the office thinks so." Her smile is fond. "He gives you special treatment."

"No, no," I say. "He's been nothing but professional."

"Yeah, right." She winks. "Like it's everyday he hands a staff member his card to shop."

I swallow. "But—"

"Nothing, darling. Enjoy being the favorite." She doesn't allow me to say more as she waves a cab down and helps me stuff the many bags in the trunk.

I get in the backseat and wave. "Thanks a lot."

"See you tomorrow." She blows me a kiss.

We drive off and I lean back, replaying her words. I'm not certain how to feel or what to do next. So I close my eyes instead and enjoy the feel of the air sweeping across my face.

Chance appears behind my eyelids, just the way he was this morning. Sitting in his office chair, looking every bit powerful and sinful with his cock sticking out of him.

There was no way I could keep myself from riding him. Even now, I press my thighs together as my imagination runs wild.

Tires screech and I'm jerked forward suddenly. The seatbelt bites into my skin and slams me back into the seat.

My eyes widen and I'm gasping for breath. "What happened?" I unclip the seat belt and lean forward.

"This car just cut in front of us," the driver complains, then devolves into a tirade.

I hear nothing as I take in the car. It's night but I can tell—the black, sleek vehicle is just like the one that trailed me earlier.

Panic sends my heart to my throat. "Drive, drive!" I pull on my driver's shoulder. "Go! Now!"

He doesn't wait for more. He reverses and cuts a wide arc around the car.

I turn in time to see a man dressed in all black getting out of the black car. There's something in his hand that looks like a fucking gun.

"Faster!" I gasp.

"Don't worry, miss. I know all the back roads they can't follow."

True to his word, the cab driver goes in circles, passing neighborhoods I've never seen before he stops in front of the Resort. There's no one following us.

For the first time since we were cut off, I take a full breath.

While the cab driver takes my stuff out of the trunk, I search my purse looking for any amount that can show my gratitude. I end up emptying it and handing over all the bills, including change.

He doesn't look at it as he collects it. "Stay safe, miss. Those men looked dangerous."

I nod shakily. "Thank you."

He gets into his car then and drives off.

I watch his headlights disappear in the distance before hefting my bags and racing to the villa.

The next morning, I find Chance in his office as early as eight a.m. His eyes lift from his laptop and then he does a double take. I'm in a matte pink dress that hugs my skin and stops just below my knees with shoes to match.

His eyes turn warm with appreciation and my belly flips in response. I picked what I liked to wear the previous night, but seeing that he likes it too causes a warm rush to flood me.

"Good morning." I place the card on the desk and slide it back. "I got all I needed, thank you."

His eyes tear away from my body and he meets my face. "Are you sure?"

What? Didn't he see the alerts of how much I spent? I keep my face serene though. "Yes."

He takes the card then and slips it into a drawer. "And you remember Sunday dinner, right?"

I nod. "Of course." I can't forget it if I tried. I'd be meeting all the Eastons. Daunting didn't begin to cover it. "And you'll tell them we're not really dating?"

He pauses. "I will."

"Okay."

"Is everything all right?" His brows furrow as I remain there.

I debate telling him about last night. I'm only here for a few weeks. If I'm careful, then I won't run into those men again.

But last night's experience left me tossing and turning until three a.m. Even now, I don't feel like myself and it took a thick layer of concealer to hide the dark circles under my eyes. I can't function in this stressed out state.

"No, it's not."

Chance is on his feet in an instant and he comes round the table to cup my face.

"Tell me. What's wrong?"

I gulp. Looking at him this close, his forehead knitted and a frown pulling his lips down, I can't help but feel he's worried about me because it's me. Will he hold his other employees so tenderly? Or would he look like he was ready to bulldoze through whatever the problem is?

"You can tell me anything, Maddie." His voice is warm and hoarse and concerned.

I break. Tears well up in my eyes, but I swallow them down.

"Someone was following me yesterday," I sound shaky, but I can't help it. I feel shaken. "In the morning on my way to work and after when Julia and I went to shop."

I explain how the cab driver saved me.

"Am I being paranoid?"

"No, you're not," Chance says firmly, thumbing my cheeks in a soothing, rhythmic way. "Why didn't you tell me when it first happened?"

"I... I didn't want to bother you. Maybe I was imagining things. I don't know."

"Never keep anything from me, okay? No matter how crazy you think it sounds."

I nod.

He turns away and picks up his phone. "I need to get someone to watch you. Make sure no one follows you and you're always safe."

"Um... is that really necessary?"

He turns to me with an anguished look on his face. "Most certainly, yes." Whoever is at the other end picks and he speaks into the phone. Almost as quickly as it started, the call ends. He places his phone back on the desk. "It's done. By evening, you'll have someone watching your back wherever you are."

I swallow. "Thank you."

He nodded firmly.

I turn to leave, but a hand on my arm stops me.

He pulls me back against his chest.

"Where do you think you're going?" His arms wrap around me, firm and comforting.

I melt into his touch, burying my face in his chest. I pull a deep breath of his coffee and coconut scent. It sends relief through my limbs.

Everything will be alright. I just know it.

Chapter Eight

Chance

I'm at Maddie's villa on Sunday evening. Seeing her every day for the past week and not yesterday has increased my craving for her. Anticipation pounds through me.

I rap at the door and wait. Thirty seconds pass before it flies open. I'm hit with her beauty like a gust of wind. I stare for a full minute before I find my voice.

"Hi."

She smiles and scrambles my brain. *Again.* "Hi."

"Hi."

Her laughter is pure honey running down my spine. "Hi?"

I clear my throat, look away for a second to get myself together. When I look back, her eyes are brown pools taking me in, trailing every length of my skin.

I dressed down for dinner in a form-fitting shirt and black jeans with boots. But she looks at me like I have no clothes on at all.

I want her with no clothes on. The temptation to rid her of the blue sundress she has on, and muss up her wavy styled hair is strong.

But that can't happen.

"You ready?"

"Yes. I'll grab my purse."

She turns around and I'm served with her shapely hips running down to slender calves.

I look away and count backward from hundred. Anything to keep me distracted.

The lock clicks and she announces, "I'm ready."

I offer her my arm and she takes it with a big smile. I'm loath to leave her side and only realize I have to when we're standing at the passenger door.

Kicking myself into action, I pull the door open and she slips in.

I get into the car next to her and head off. Her gaze is fixed outside the window, giving me the opportunity to really look at her.

I can't believe I'm bringing her home to my family.

Excitement threads through me and I have to force myself to slow down. She's smart, funny and beautiful. Everyone will be thrilled to meet her.

You'll tell them we're not really dating.

The promise she asked of me circles my thoughts. I have to tell them.

Baxter's smug satisfaction flashes in my head and I grit my teeth. He's going to mock and say he knew it all along. He's going to want Maddie when he learns the truth.

I turn to look at her once more and she's watching me.

"Is something wrong?" she asks.

I shake my head.

Whatever she sees on my face makes her look into the rearview mirror, then her side mirror.

Anger surges like a live wire inside me. She's worried about being followed.

It didn't cross my mind because I trust the men I employed to watch her.

They reported that they indeed spotted a suspicious black car. They've been following it to ferret out who they are and what they want. So far, they have nothing on those two key details because they always miss the men.

But none of them have come close to hurting Maddie like that night and that is the most important thing to me.

Still, I slow down and scan the areas behind us. She'd described the car as black with tinted windows.

There are no black cars coming up behind us. The only one is ahead and when I drive past it, it's a couple and their kid.

Maddie relaxes and I calm down too.

Even if someone was after her, as long as she's with me, I'd never let anyone hurt her.

I turn down the lane that leads to Dad's house and Maddie sits up.

"Where are we?"

I smile. The mansion is tucked in the middle of acres and acres of land we explored as children. I can see how it'd awe someone from the city.

"This belongs to your family?" she mutters.

I nod. Her *wow* is more breathed than spoken and it satisfies me that I can share the beauty with her.

I turn into the final stretch and we pull up to the house. It's closed off by a wrought iron gate. Once the security cameras spot my car, though, the gate opens and we drive through.

I stop next to Baxter's Porsche and I'm on guard immediately. He's probably here so early to stir up trouble before Maddie and I show up.

With a bit of effort, I push away thoughts of my troublesome brother as Maddie and I exit the car. She spends a minute taking in the environment underneath the setting sun.

I'm focused on her instead.

Finally, she meets my eyes. "Can we go in now?"

"Of course."

I lead us up the steps to the front door and knock.

Almost immediately, the door opens. And it's none other than Baxter. Why am I not surprised?

His smile grows wider as his eyes fall on us. "Right on time you two." He nods at me. "Brother." Then turns to Maddie. "Miss Lowe."

"Baxter! It's great to see you again."

"And you too." He flashes a practiced grin at her.

"Good. We're all happy to see ourselves." I place a hand on Maddie's lower back to steer her away, but Baxter blocks our path.

"Whoa. Calm down, big guy. What's the hurry? I'm still saying hi to Maddie."

"Hi is a single word and you've said so."

"Not to me it isn't." He winks, then turns to Maddie. "Hello, again. For some reason Chance doesn't want me to say hi to you. Think that's fair?"

Maddie shakes her head, her eyes sympathetic. "Nah."

"Right? I thought so too." His eyes sweep over her. "By the way, you look so gorgeous! What?!"

Maddie laughs. "Yeah, right. You're the one sporting all the bling." She points to the single diamond stud in his left ear.

He waves a hand and bows his head as though he's shy, but I know he's eating up all the attention with glee.

I bristle. Why are we doing this anyway?

"No, that's all you Miss Lowe. You're practically glowing." He slaps a hand on my shoulder.

I glare at him but he doesn't take it off.

"Didn't Chance tell you?"

Her smile withers. She opens her mouth and shuts it, then glances away.

And I realize.

I didn't actually say so. I was floored at her beauty. I was amazed, but I never mentioned it.

Shit. Did she think I didn't think so? Because I do. So fucking much.

But unlike Baxter who spins words like a poet, I'm the opposite. I say facts and that's all. Telling her she's simply beautiful is inadequate. I want to say more, to do more.

And now she won't look my way.

Baxter looks between us, his eyes twinkling. "Maybe he was saving it for later tonight?" He bumps my shoulder with a closed fist. "Right, bro?"

I eye him. This wouldn't have come up if he didn't meddle. "Yeah. Right."

He ignores my annoyance and spins to Maddie. "I've told everyone about you and they are all excited." He gives her his arm. "Come right away! Come and meet everyone."

Maddie throws me a glance before slipping her hand into the curve of Baxter's arm.

He whisks her away, giving her a tour of the house as they go.

I shut the door behind myself, my eyes still glued on where Baxter is acting as though Maddie is his.

She glances over her shoulder, a small smile playing on her lips and I'm consoled a bit.

She's still mine. My fake girlfriend, but my girlfriend nonetheless. He wouldn't dare go there.

He wouldn't.

With that, I peel myself away from the entrance and join the rest of the family.

Chapter Nine

Maddie

Voices filter out from an open door and my fingers dig into Baxter's arm on reflex. He smiles down at me and pats the back of my hand reassuringly.

"Come on, I'll show you the living room." He drags me away from the voices to a high-ceilinged room. There's a floor length window overlooking a garden fresh with greenery.

"It's so beautiful," I breathe.

"It is." He steers me toward a mantle over a fireplace. "These are even more beautiful."

I lean in and squint at the photos. It's easy to make out Chance's teenage face. He hasn't changed much, scowl and all. There's just light in his young eyes that I don't see now.

I back away, uncertain if he'd like me looking at those photos. I'm only his employee and fake girlfriend. By the end of the night, I won't be one of those anymore.

I shouldn't get intimate with his life.

Baxter takes me to more parts of the house, showing me dents in the wall he and Chance made when roughhousing.

"There were three of you in the photo?" I prompt.

"Oh, yeah. Our little brother, Landon. He'll be at dinner tonight. You'll get to meet him too."

By the time the downstairs tour is over, I'm feeling less nervous at the prospect of meeting the family. Baxter smiles knowingly. He did the tour to allow me to calm down and prepare myself.

I'm about to say a *thank you* when Chance comes out of the kitchen carrying a tray. His eyes drift over Baxter and I, then latch onto the place where my hand meets his brother's arm.

His look darkens and I have the impulse to remove my hand. I resist though, and look at him askance.

"Dinner's ready," is all he says and goes ahead into the dining room.

"Shall we?" Baxter inclines his head, his smile still on despite Chance's attitude.

"Yes."

"Sure?"

I have the distinct feeling he won't push it if I need more time to get ready. But I smile. "I'm ready, thank you."

"It's no problem at all." He gestures toward the door. "This way, Miss Lowe."

We walk through the door and instantly, the chatter ceases.

All gazes focus on Baxter and me. No, not Baxter who's shadowing me. They're all looking much lower at me.

I gulp.

Baxter places a supportive hand on my shoulder. "Everyone, meet Miss Maddie Lowe."

"Just Maddie," I add.

The girl next to an older lady quirks a smile.

"Meet Just Maddie," Baxter amends to a few chuckles—none from Chance. "And Maddie, this is my dad, Dan Easton."

Dan rises and I'm forced to cross the room and take the hand he stretches out.

Dan's handshake is firm and his smile warm. "Welcome to our home, Maddie."

"Thank you, sir." I sound breathless.

"Not sir. Just Dan."

"Just Dan?"

"Yes."

"Okay, Just Dan."

His smile grows and his eyes crinkle. He lets my hand go as Baxter introduces the next people at the table.

"This is our Aunt Felicia. And her daughter, Lucy, our cousin." He ruffles Lucy's hair to which she yells and rises to play-punch him.

I greet Aunt Felicia and she smiles.

"Lovely to have you, Maddie. I hope you like a good spicy chicken. I make the best."

"It's one of my favorites."

When Lucy manages to subdue Baxter, she turns to me with a wide grin.

"Welcome to the family!"

Before I can amend that I'm not actually part of the family yet. Or ever will be.

She hugs me. Tight.

"I'm so happy Chance found you."

I hug her back but look over her shoulder to meet Chance's eyes. I'd hate to break their hearts, but I don't fit in their world. They'd soon realize that and want me gone anyway.

It's best to end things now before I get any closer to them.

"And one more person." Baxter pulls me away from Lucy's hug and gives her the stink eye.

She returns it with equal fervency.

I smile, sure I'm going to love her.

"This is Landon. Our baby brother."

He's certainly not a baby. Even sitting, he looks as tall as Chance and Baxter but without a similar build.

He's on his iPad typing furiously and doesn't look up until Baxter taps his shoulder.

His gaze shoots up and I'm hit with the intensity of it. Clear blue eyes search my face and then he says, "Nice to have you here, Maddie."

"Nice to be here..." He goes back to his iPad. "...too."

What was that? I turn to Baxter for an explanation but he only shrugs with a smile.

He leads me on and deposits me in the empty chair next to Chance.

"Your family is very nice," I tell Chance.

"Yep." His eyes follow Baxter as he rounds the table to take the spot opposite us next to Lucy.

Baxter meets his older brother's eyes and winks.

I can't help my chuckle. For some reason, Baxter enjoys teasing Chance and Chance always falls for it.

I glance sideways at Chance and before everyone else, he starts to dish his meal, his motions stiff.

He's slapping on mashed potatoes now. I touch his arm and he turns my way.

With a small smile, I take the spoon from him and do it myself. He lets me.

The slight shake in my hand is definitely not because he's looking at me.

Once everyone's plates are full, we dig in. It's delicious and I tell Aunt Felicia.

She beams. "That's Sunday dinner for you, my dear. Next Sunday I'm trying out these Mexican dishes that are oh so delicious. You won't believe your tongue when you taste them. I've never tried the recipes but on my last vacation to Mexico, the yacht chef made them and I have to try them."

"Hey, mom." Lucy drops the wineglass she's sipping from. "Didn't you try those recipes you got from the Bahamas that one time and it was a disaster?"

Baxter snickers.

Aunt Felicia throws him a stern look, then directs the same at Lucy. "You both have bad taste." She turns to Chance. "Tell Maddie how good it was."

"It was good," Chance says.

Lucy rolls her eyes. "Chance doesn't want to hurt your feelings, that's all. Uncle Dan, wasn't the food awful?"

Dan shakes his head and points at his mouth signaling he has a mouthful and can't talk.

Lucy laughs. She faces me. "Uncle Dan doesn't lie, unlike Chance. So he'd rather say nothing."

Dan sips from his glass and finally speaks, "It was different."

"That's code for bad, but he's trying to be nice," Lucy says.

"Fine." Aunt Felicia rolls her eyes. "That was that recipe but I promise next Sunday's will be excellent! You'll be here for that, right?" She looks at me enthusiastically.

"Um..." I glance sideways at Chance.

"Can we eat up this delicious meal first before talking about what will happen next week?" Chance says.

Aunt Felicia smiles. "Of course."

She's probably pleased he complimented the meal.

"So, Maddie," Lucy chirps, "Where are you from?"

"Let Maddie eat, will you?" Chance smiles tightly.

"I didn't..."

Chance interrupts with work talk directed at Dan, effectively stamping out Lucy's line of questioning. Maybe he doesn't want them finding out I'm a nobody. Or he doesn't want more about me to be said because by dinner's end, it'll be over.

Either way, it hurts. I know we shouldn't dive deeper into each other's lives. But despite my nerves earlier on, I'm comfortable around the Eastons.

I move around my meal until Dan shifts away the conversation from work. Then I perk up.

"When were you going to bring Maddie for us to meet her?" Dan asks. "If Baxter didn't say anything, we would have still been in the dark about your girlfriend."

Chance glances at me. "I was waiting for the right time."

"Well, better late than never!"

"Yeah sure, dad." Chance resumes eating.

"I mean, I never thought I'd see you with a woman. You act like you're married to your work. Working so hard."

"For the family." Chance's voice is cold and detached. "It's what we have to do, right?"

"Not have to." Dan leans forward, his eyes glued on Chance even though Chance's gaze is fixed on his nearly empty plate. "Work is work and there's life outside of that."

"I have a life outside of work."

"Well, thank heavens for Maddie because—"

"Even before Maddie, I did." Chance's gaze shoots up to his dad and the table goes quiet.

My gaze shifts between everyone as I try to understand what's going on. Is this something they've spoken about before? It seems there's an underlying tension and I'm not sure what it is.

"Well, let's agree to disagree, eh?" Dan smiles and in the moment, he reminds of Baxter. Chance doesn't reply and he continues, "I'm just so glad you brought Maddie to us today. We are very happy to have her." He faces me. "And you're always welcome."

Crap.

I smile. "Thank you."

We're going to break their hearts when we say it's not real.

I go back to eating, dreading the moment Chance decides to finally speak up. The only thing I'm grateful for is that in two weeks, I'd be out of Magic Island and never have to see these kind people I lied to ever again.

But dinner's getting to a close and Chance isn't saying a word.

I'm enjoying my ice cream and cake dessert and giving him the side eye he completely misses.

"Chance?" I say finally, pressing out a smile and moving my eyes in a way that says tell them, I hope.

His eyes dim. He gets it. Good.

I wait, the ice cream on my tongue turning to sawdust. I'm not sure how they'd react but I hope it won't be yelling-level bad. I look around the table and I'm sure it won't go that far. They're nice people.

Chance clears his throat. He looks at me, and then scans the table. From Landon whose face is buried in his iPad, to Lucy who's chatting with Baxter and Aunt Felicia who's topping up Dan's dessert plate.

It's a struggle for him. He probably didn't think it'd be hard.

I place my hand on his for support. When his warm fingers cover mine, I almost melt. We sat together all night but barely touched each other.

This feels good. Right.

NO.

It ends now.

Tell them, Chance. I plead with my eyes.

"Dad and... everyone."

They all turn to him.

I hold my breath and keep my gaze down.

His fingers thread mine. "Maddie and I... we work together."

Okay...

Say *so we cannot date*.

"Baxter mentioned it." Dan's voice.

So we cannot date!

"Yeah, and it's been great so far. She's really competent at her job. In fact, she poked holes in Ramsey's plans on her first day."

"He's always too cocky," Dan says. "But you know, one in five of his attempts work so he stays on."

Chance continues. "Of course. His recent campaign covering..."

I look up at Chance, my mouth threatening to hang loose. What the fuck? I thought he was going to say it and now he's talking about work?

I poke his side with an elbow.

He huffs and looks my way. I eyeball him and he shrugs. *Shrugs!*

I press my mouth shut and face forward. Baxter's looking between us, his eyes narrowed but I don't care.

I'm mad at Chance for not following through and forcing us to continue this charade.

I'm mad I played along in the first place.

And I'm mad at myself for being unable to repress my shiver as he leans in to whisper in my ear.

Whatever he says, I don't hear it. Too mad and too turned on for my own good.

Damn him.

Chapter Ten

Chance

Maddie walks into my office on Monday morning and slams the files I requested on my desk. Before I can speak, she shoots off outlining the stuff I have to attend to for the day.

"Maddie?"

"Want some coffee?" she snaps. "I can get you coffee and I'll do it right away. I'll go to the break room, make a nice cup and bring it back and hand it to you, still steaming because I do what I say I'll do."

"Coffee sounds nice, but—"

"What, sir?"

"Maddie, calm down."

"Oh, I'm calm. Now, would that be all? Well, thank you. I'll be somewhere else doing stuff with people who can follow through!"

She spins around and flounces to the door. I don't think she intends the sway of her hips to be enticing, but it is.

The door shuts, cutting off my view of her and bringing my head back to why she's so mad.

I didn't tell my family what we agreed on.

I groan and rise, going to look out the window.

How do I explain it to her? It'd require coming clean, telling her everything but I could never. She'd look at me differently, hate me.

I can't bear that.

Dad almost let it slip last night and I'm glad he didn't.

But I also can't forget the look on his face, the pride and joy.

I work myself to the bone to keep the Island as one of the most successful this side of the globe and Dad's approval has always been half-hearted at best.

But bringing home a woman? That pleased him a lot.

It pleased all of them.

Even Landon came up to see Maddie speak a few times. He stayed throughout dinner—something he never did. Then he waved and near-smiled as she left.

Just one night and she'd found her way into Dad's heart and became accepted as one of us.

When she asked me to say it, tell them it isn't real and she would be leaving, I couldn't. Throughout the dinner, I dreaded the moment I had to.

And when the moment came, I closed up.

I failed her.

Her attitude is completely understood. I earned that.

She didn't speak to me on the ride back to the villa, her gaze firmly out the window. My goodnight was returned with a slammed door to my face.

Why did I think she'd let it go in the morning?

She's even more pissed off.

I have some apologizing to do.

I can't work with her mad at me. I don't want her saying or doing something to get the staff talking. My relationship with Maddie is none of their business, and I'm eager to keep it private.

I press the intercom. "Julia, send in Maddie."

I stand facing the door and moments later, she walks in.

Her eyes snag on mine and narrow with annoyance.

I cross the room to stand before her.

"Maddie, I understand that you're angry—"

"No, you don't!" she snaps, tearing away from my side and stomping over to my desk.

I turn in time to get a glimpse of her ass and I stifle a groan.

She spins around. "You lied to me."

"No." I step forward. "I didn't lie. I'd never lie to you. I meant to tell them but... but..."

"But what?" she challenges. "What part of Maddie is, in fact, not my girlfriend, is so hard, huh?"

I look down and exhale before meeting her eyes again. There's no use cooking up tales. She deserves the truth.

"I'm fucking 37, Maddie, and I don't date. I do nothing outside of work. Work is my life."

Her face softens. She's probably remembering Dad's ribbing last night.

I let her mull on that before I continue, "They've never seen me with a woman before and to them, it's a big deal. I didn't know they were going to take it so seriously, but they have."

"So you're going to allow them to keep believing that when it's not serious? Hell, it's not even real!" She gestures between us, her features pinched. "This doesn't exist. I'm going back and you're going to continue being here. Being... you." She swallows thickly and I'm not sure it's only last night that is the problem anymore.

I close the distance between us as she looks away and catches her breath.

She faces me again, her eyes sad. "Your family's great and I understand that you don't want to disappoint them. But keeping up the lie is worse."

"I know, but what they don't know won't hurt them, right?"

She starts to shake her head and look away but I cup her face and turn her back to look at me.

"I know you don't like this, but I don't want to break my dad's heart. I just want them to be happy, even if it's only for a while."

"What are you saying?" Her eyes turn hazy as I work a couple fingers into the hair at her nape. It's soft and curls around my fingers.

"I'm saying..." My throat closes up as her mouth parts. "I'm saying I need you to say you'll be my fake girlfriend for the rest of the time that you'll be here."

Her eyes widen. "You want us to keep pretending."

"Yes."

"But..."

I add both middle fingers to the ones caressing her scalp and she moans softly.

Fuck. The sound is like a trigger to my cock. I step closer so her supple body is pressed up against mine.

"Mhm?" I prompt, eager to see those lips part once more, form words, say stuff to me.

"You're confusing me with your touch," she whispers.

"It's not intentional, I promise."

"Hmm..." she says. "Yeah, well. I like it."

I smile down at her smooth features.

"You know what? Okay, let's do it."

"You'll be my girlfriend?"

"Fake girlfriend." Her eyes snap open. "That's all it is."

"Yes, ma'am."

She pulls out of my hold and I frown.

"What are you doing?"

"Trying to explain to you." She only stops when her backside hits the desk. "Since I'm going to be acting the part of your girlfriend, we have to keep things... platonic."

I swallow my groan. "Platonic?"

She licks her lip, her gaze dropping to my chest, then back up. "Yeah."

"You mean I can't fuck you and make you cum on my cock?"

Her eyes widen, her nostrils flared. "Yes, people who are on platonic terms don't do that. We can't allow the lines to get blurred. It has to be clear what we are."

"I'm clear on that." I close in on her, placing both hands on the desk, caging her in.

I lean down so our faces are level, and I don't miss the excitement bouncing in her eyes.

"I understand that you're my girlfriend."

"Fake," she says faintly, breathlessly.

"Of course." I press my nose to the curve of her neck and drink in her flowery fragrance.

She shivers and a hand flies up to my chest. I'm certain she'll push me away, but her fingers dig into my skin instead.

A savage smile tilts my lips. She wants me as much as I want her.

"I understand too that I'm the only one who makes you cum so hard you tremble."

"No, you don't." She's breathless with desire but still so stubborn. "We can't."

I tongue the quivering pulse at the base of her neck and her body curves into mine. Her head falls back and she whimpers.

"You sure about that, Maddie?"

She uses both hands to grip the back of my neck, pulling me lower.

I'm powerless to resist the invitation. I press open mouth kisses to her soft skin, sucking on the tender flesh.

She whimpers, her fingers pulling at my hair, roping down my back, her legs unsteady.

I come up for air and meet languid eyes.

She drags me back down so our mouths collide. I taste her and I'm gone.

There's nothing else I'd rather do.

Her tongue tangles with mine and I suck on it, wrapping her up in my arms and bringing her closer so we're chest to chest. Her legs widen to accommodate me between her thighs.

My hands wander and touch the smooth flesh of her exposed thighs and I groan.

I tear my mouth from hers and meet her heavy-lidded eyes.

"I don't—we shouldn't be doing this," she says, but she's unbuttoning my shirt and pushing slender fingers inside to touch my skin.

"I know." I kiss her lips, just a quick taste but I'm tempted to keep going. I suck on her lower lip and say between ragged breaths, "Just this once. One last time and never again."

She gives in with a stuttered moan. "Yes, yes."

I peel her hands from my body and pin them behind her. "Lean back."

She obeys and I'm free to explore her.

I unbutton her blouse and a black bra hides her tits from me. Impatient, I tug it down and red rosy nipples pop out. Hard and pointy.

I lick the left one, then the right, unable to choose which to stick to.

She's writhing, shaking.

I snake my arms around her hips to hold her steady. Her fingers find my hair and clutch.

I'm certain it'll look a mess afterward. I still have meetings to attend, investors to meet. But I don't care.

In fact, I want them to suspect. Want them to see her flushed and me mussed up.

I kiss down her trembling belly to the center of her thighs.

Her skirt is trapped around her waist so it takes nothing to slide down her panties. I'm favored with her glistening slit and a thatch of warm brown hair.

I'm panting as I lean in and tongue her open.

She moans loudly, falling back against the desk.

She's completely open before me now. Both legs spread, pussy lips opening up like flower petals about to be bathed with sunlight.

My cock aches to slide into her wetness, but not yet.

Must give her pleasure first.

Shutting my eyes, I savor her taste with licks, kisses and sucks.

She's crazy for it, trembling and screaming my name, her fingers pulling at my hair.

"Fuck me, Chance, please."

I slip a finger into her channel and stroke.

"More, more," she cries.

So I add a second finger and her back bows. I know it's good but not nearly enough to bring her to completion, so I find her clit.

It's pink and swollen and sticking out, begging to be kissed. I suck it into my mouth and roll my tongue around it. It takes a few seconds to find the spot that'd make her scream but once I do, she doesn't disappoint.

She bucks up to meet my ministrations, her hips rolling around, covering my lower face in her juices. Nothing ever tasted this good.

I palm my cock through my slacks, groaning, turned on to my limit as I give her pleasure. I'm nearly busting when she spasms around my fingers. My need is on the backburner now as I stretch her pleasure.

She whines, her body stiff. Shivers wrack through her and I hold steady, giving long licks to her pleasure spot.

She falls back against the desk with a sigh and I lick up the last of her satisfaction.

I stand over her, pleased at her languid smile as tremors still rock her.

"We're not done yet."

Her smile grows wider and she lifts her hips, offering her sweet pussy to me.

Fuck. I can't get my zipper off fast enough.

Before my slacks can hit the floor, I'm inside her.

She accepts me with a soft moan, her eyes fanning shut. I bend over, going deeper. I want to go slow, make this moment last, but it's impossible. She's too warm and wet and unreal.

I'm unable to hold back.

Bracing my hands on the desk, I fuck her. Hard.

She receives it with eager whimpers and I can't stop. Not until I bathe her walls with my cum and she's mine.

I shut down the voice in my head telling me I'm wrong. She'll never be mine.

I close the space between us and rock my hips in just the right way to stimulate her clit. Before long, she's wracked with a fresh wave of shivers and she's milking my cock.

I empty inside her, my eyes blind with satisfaction. We rock against each other until we're powerless to keep moving.

I sag against her, spreading soft kisses across her face.

We have to clean up and return to our duties, but for now, I'm content to just hold her.

Chapter Eleven

Maddie

I have my feet up on the coffee table and my hair in a loose bun. Cozy pajamas hug my skin and a cool breeze filters across my neck from the open window. I'm catching up with work I didn't do earlier today because... well... I got carried away with my boss.

Warmth curls in my belly even as the memory of what we did aches between my thighs.

It's the last time, right? No use dwelling on it. Except, that's all I can think about. All I've been able to since the moment his fingers dug into my skin and he sunk himself deep inside me.

I lean back on the backrest, eyes closed, body tingling.

Maybe I can take a short break and fix the growing ache between my legs.

My phone rings.

Ugh, no. I like my daydreams about Chance better, so I ignore it.

It cuts and starts up again. Whoever it is must *really* want to talk. Sighing, I reach across the table and pick it up.

It's Nat.

My horniness fades as I swipe to answer. "Hey."

"Were you in a meeting? Is that why you didn't take your call?"

"What? At ten p.m.?"

"What do I know? CEOs are popular for working their employees too hard."

I say nothing. He did work me hard, but not in the way Nat means.

"Maddie?"

"Yeah. How's everything with you?"

"Babes, I miss you. But tell me everything! How's Magic Island and working with the super sexy Chance Easton?"

We sent texts back and forth over the past few days, but no talks yet.

I blush. "Um, it's good."

"Just good." Her tone is suspicious. "Sounds like there's more. Is there something you're not telling me?"

"What? No!" I'm high-pitched, but I can't help it.

"Maddie..."

"Fine," I sigh. "Something happened."

There's shuffling from Nat's end. She's most likely settling in to get the tea.

"Are you done?"

She laughs. "Almost. And... Now, I'm done. Tell me everything."

"I slept with Chance."

She gasps. "What?"

"Twice."

"*What?!*"

"I messed up, I know. Between the girlfriend thing and this, things might get a little confusing."

"Mads, I'd smack you upside the head if I were there."

My shoulders fall. "I know. It's getting to be a shit show right now. But we agreed that today was the last time and—"

"You will do no such thing!"

"What?"

Nat groans. "Maddie Lowe, what am I going to do with you?"

"What are you talking about?"

"Um, you're fucking a billionaire and meeting his family? What does that say about you and him?"

"Nat, we're not an item. We were pretty clear on that. And I'm leaving in two weeks. And I don't like him like that."

"Uh-huh."

"I mean it!"

"And I completely believe you."

"Ugh, you'll see. Enough about me, what's going on with you?"

"Work, partying, the usual. Oh, and there's more."

My brows furrow. "More like?"

"I saw Todd. Twice."

My heart doesn't skip a beat or tremble. I have zero reaction to that information.

"And?"

"He asked how you're doing."

"Oh, did he? That's cute."

"He wonders when you'll come back so you both can make up."

I throw my head back and laugh. "Yeah, right. Like that would ever happen."

"I told him the same. Guess he's hoping for a miracle."

"Never happening," I say, feeling nothing at all.

"I'm a hundred percent with you on that. Especially now that you're getting it from a hot billionaire."

"I kinda regret telling you he's rich," I deadpan.

Nat keeps cheering. "Mads, honey, wouldn't you rather be with a rich guy with a great family than... Todd."

I chuckle. "I would rather, but that isn't happening."

"You don't know that."

"I do. And you need to stop hinting at something more. I'm a fake girlfriend and we've done the deed twice only and we made a pact that we won't anymore."

Nat yawns. "Are you done?"

"Oh, so now I'm boring you?"

"Yes! Your pessimism is sleep-inducing."

"Whatever. I'm speaking the truth though."

"Keep telling yourself that."

"I will."

"Every morning."

"I do."

"That you like him and he likes you."

"I do—No, wait! That's not—"

Nat cackles. "You admitted it!"

"I hate you."

"I love you." She smacks kisses into the phone which makes me smile. "Got to go. We'll talk soon, okay? So you can tell me about more sexy times between you and Mr. Easton. About all the times he touches you—"

"No, no! Bye, Nat." I disconnect the call just as she goes into graphic detail.

Despite myself, I smile.

There's no way this thing between Chance and I would live beyond my few weeks on the Island. Heck, he never even implied he wanted anything more.

Nat is crazy. And I'm not. So I'm keeping the boundaries clear and protecting my heart. Hell, when it comes to Chance, I have no heart.

There.

I push away the thoughts Nat planted in my head and focus on rounding up with work. It takes thirty minutes to wrap up.

I close my laptop and stretch, then rub at my eyes. If I'm to make it to work early, I need to be in bed ASAP.

Up on my feet, I make sure the doors are locked and I shut the window, then I head over to the bedroom where my fluffy bed awaits.

I curl up underneath the covers and wait for blissful sleep. It comes easily, taking away my consciousness and pulling me into a dreamlike state.

And then I hear it.

Something scratches against metal or... glass?

I roll over and tuck myself deeper, determined not to lose the threads of sleep weaving over me.

But the sound persists.

Then a crack.

My eyes split open. It's dark and quiet in my room. Except for the creaky sound now. It cuts through the silence and arrows fear into my heart.

What if they've come for me?

That thought jerks me up and I scan the dark. I scramble sideways and slap a hand on the nightstand lamp. It illuminates the room in a warm glow that reveals I'm alone.

But I know what I heard.

Heart trembling, I climb off the bed and turn in a slow circle. "W-who's there?"

No answer.

My eyes snag on the slightly open window. I inch toward it. A soft breeze tickles the hairs hanging down my cheeks.

Did I leave it open?

I don't remember. I only remember shutting the window in the living room.

Swallowing, I push it open and lean out. There's nothing to the night but the green garden and the trees. And a tree branch hanging so close to the window. That must be where the scratchy sound came from.

I pull the window back into place and slide the lock in place, then I pad over to my bed and climb in.

My eyes stay open for the next five minutes as I listen out for any suspicious sounds.

There are none.

Slowly, I put off the lamp and tuck myself in again. This time, sleep doesn't come easily.

I'm working late on a Tuesday night.

It's not because of the trouble I had sleeping the previous night or anything. I've since concluded that the noise at the window came from the tree branch and the wind, plus my overactive imagination.

I'm not scared of going home and being alone there.

Julia left two hours ago and since then, the office has grown quieter. I should leave too. I've already fixed the calendar five days ahead and cleaned up Chance's notes. There's nothing left to do.

Inhale, exhale. I can do this.

Nothing can hurt you, Maddie.

With that thought locked in place, I pack up my purse and head out. I'm walking past Chance's office when I spy a light coming through the door.

Frowning, I head toward it. Did he forget to turn off the switch when he left?

I always leave before him so I don't know what happens after.

I pause by the door, then push it open.

Chance is behind his desk, eyes glued on a document he's holding before him. "Just an hour more, Freddy."

That's the night guard.

"It isn't Freddy."

Chance's face comes up. "Oh." His gaze sweeps over me. "What are you doing here?"

"I was heading home when I saw the light on in your office. I assumed you forgot to turn it off."

He smirks. "I don't. Why haven't you gone home?"

He already has men protecting me. I don't need him to get worried about every creak and rattle that startles me. Plus, it was *nothing*.

"Just working." I shrug. "What are you doing?"

"Working, too."

"On what at this time of the night?" I glance at my watch. "Eight-thirty!"

"I could ask you the same."

I eye him, inching into his office. The door clips shut behind me as I draw close to his desk.

I don't miss the way his eyes follow my movements. Watching, assessing. Almost like a predator onto a prey.

And why does that thought leave a delicious tingle down my spine?

I stop before his desk and focus on the papers covering the expansive surface. "What are these?"

"Progress reports dating back many years."

"'20s?" I frown at the brown piece of paper. "Why would you need this?"

"We learn from the past to fix the present, don't we?"

"Huh. So what are you learning?" I round the desk to take a peek at the notes he's making.

His handwriting is messy but familiar. I don't pay too much attention, though, as I focus on the notes he's taking.

"'Cutting employees reduced productivity and affected income generation'." I run a finger down the page, reading more of the notes. By the time I'm done, I turn to see Chance watching me carefully.

His dark brown hair is mussed from a long work day and his eyes are lined. Even so, he looks so good my heart quickens.

I drop my gaze and my eyes snag on the undone buttons on his chest, showcasing smooth tan skin. Then lower to his rolled-up sleeves and corded forearms.

I swallow. "These are... interesting." My voice is squeaky! Why is it squeaky?

If my boss notices, he doesn't draw attention to it. "They are. It's the trends that matter. The highs and lows of the Island's businesses, the growth of its population, or the downturn of the same is traceable to policies my grandfather and father put in place." He sighs and leans back, looking at the spread of papers. "I want to learn from them and make Magic Island the best it can be in my time."

My brows furrow as I watch him. I can't imagine what it means to be tasked with looking over a company, much less be the deciding voice in what happens on a whole Island.

"You're doing great."

He chuckles and looks up at me, his eyes vulnerable. "Am I?"

I squeeze my hand into a fist, resisting the urge to run my fingers through his hair.

"You are. It's quite obvious your family is proud of you." He's still doubtful, so I press on. "My parents are the opposite. My dad would ask me why I'm not doing more and my mom would be overly concerned that I'm doing anything at all."

He smiles, one of the very few I've ever seen. "I don't know what my mom would think."

Since he brought it up... "Why's that?"

His eyes refocus and his smile drops. "Why's what?"

"You mentioned your mom? So I'm wondering why you won't know what she thinks."

A frown lines his forehead and he sits up. "I should get back to work."

He starts fiddling with the papers, his jaw set in a firm line.

What just happened?

"Oh, I..."

"You should go home." His tone is firm, all the warmth from earlier gone. "We have an early start tomorrow."

"Okay." I'm at the door when I look back. He's as I found him, only this time, his face looks troubled.

I close the door on my way out.

I stand outside the building waiting for a cab but seconds later, a car I recognize stops before me.

The window rolls down and Ralph leans out. "The boss asked me to drop you off."

I glare up at his lighted window. After dismissing me so rudely! I get into the car. Even annoyed, I'm still aware that I'm being followed and this is the safest way home.

Chapter Twelve

Maddie

Julia isn't at her desk the next morning. Just when I need her the most.

I make my way to my conference room slash shared office with three other co-workers. They're in and we exchange quick greetings before I take my seat and start work.

But I'm unable to keep my head on work. Last night is still heavy on my mind. And I thought to find Julia early today so she catches me up on the missing pieces of the Easton puzzle.

It can't be a coincidence the way Chance shut down last night. Something must have happened—something that could switch his moods so suddenly. Something involving his mom.

I sift through my memories. I was too nervous to study the photos on the mantle the day Baxter took me on the tour of their dad's home. There must have been a woman—their mom—and I missed it.

Ugh.

Unable to sit still, I shut my laptop and go in search of Julia again. She's not at her desk so I walk up and down the floor.

Luckily, I catch her on her way out of the CFO's office. She's grumbling under her breath about bosses and their stressful demands.

"Hey."

"Oh, hey, Maddie." She turns to me with a small smile. "What's up?"

I hurry to keep up with her long strides. "I have some questions but it looks like you don't have the time."

She smiles tightly and waves the stack of papers in her hands. "Not really."

"Well, then. I think my questions about Chance just have to wait."

She halts and spins to face me. "Personal questions?"

I bite back my smile, knowing I've caught her attention. "Yep."

"Come on." She pulls me into an office and shuts the door behind us.

"Whose office is this?" I stagger to a stop.

"The head of sales."

My eyes widen. I've had a run-in with the woman and she's stern. I don't want to be caught dead in her office. "Julia, not here! She'll—"

"Don't worry." She waves her hand carelessly. "She always has ten minutes of gossiping time with the CFO every morning. I left her in his office. She won't be here anytime soon."

"If you say so." I glance at the door. "I just think, what if she shows up?"

"Maddie, spill your questions. If you don't we'll be caught for real."

"Fine." I draw closer to Julia and lean in. "I don't want to be nosy but—"

"You're about to be, got it!" Julia nods with an encouraging smile.

"Okay. So last night I was talking with Chance…"

"Was this after everyone left the building and it was just the two of you?"

"Julia." I slap her arm. "Focus."

"What?" She shrugs with a big grin. "I've had my suspicions. So it's a simple yes or no."

"I have no idea what you're referring to."

"Come on." She wiggles her brows. "After work, quiet building, you're all alone, inhibitions are low…"

"Nothing happened," I say firmly, because last night, it didn't.

Her mischievous smile wanes. "You're so boring."

"Thank you. My question is this: what happened to Chance's mom? I've met his brothers and his dad but not her." I want to tell her about Chance's reaction last night but that feels too private.

"You've met the whole family? When?"

Oh, shit. I didn't tell her about the girlfriend thing. That was Nat. Before I can think of a plausible reason that's not the truth, she raises a hand.

"Hold that thought, though." She glances at the wall clock. "Madam Sales will be back soon."

I refuse to let my nerves about that get in the way. "Mm-hm," I prompt.

"Chance's mom is dead."

My heart drops into my stomach. "What?"

Nat nods. "Everyone knows it. She's been gone for many years. Close to fifteen, if I have my facts correct."

"Oh. That's... sad."

"Yep."

But it's also been so long. I have no idea what it means to lose a parent, but Nat does since her dad passed on when she was in high school. Yet, she speaks about him without growing sad.

Why did Chance react that way?

"Do you know what happened to her?"

"I heard she was diabetic and that's what killed her."

"That's all?"

Julia frowns. "Yes. Is something wrong?"

I shake my head quickly. "No, I'm just curious."

"Oops." Julia catches my arm and pulls me toward the door. "Time's up."

We're rounding the corner when I see the head of sales coming from the other direction.

Her eyes meet mine and I tear my gaze away and hurry to keep up with Julia. "There's no way she'd know we've been in her office, right?" I whisper.

"Of course not." She leans into me and sniffs.

"What are you doing?"

"Just smelling you."

"And?" I eye her profile.

"I'm just saying the only way you'll get into trouble is if she smells you in her office."

"What?"

"Your perfume stands out."

"No." I lift the curve of my inner elbow to my nose. "It does not."

"That's how I know you and"—she sends a gaze around us as if to make sure we're out of earshot—"the boss are getting cozy."

"We're not." Can she tell?

She turns with a smile. "Well, that was worth a shot."

"Julia!" I play-punch her arm. "You made that up."

"Ow." She laughs and rubs the spot. "I'm just curious, that's all."

"Well, don't be. Nothing is happening." *Anymore.*

We stop at her desk and she takes a seat. "Oh, he's here." She picks up the file he must have kept and flips through it. "Look here. He's asking for his very special PA. He can't start his day without seeing her." She wiggles her brows.

"That's a lie." I turn away before she can see my flushed face.

Her laughter trails me as I head back to the conference room.

I sit and round up with my work. Then I have to see him.

It takes forever to get to his office door because I'm walking so slowly. I sigh and push the door open.

He's behind his desk, looking sharp in a tan shirt. His gaze lifts as the door clicks shut behind me.

I look away, guilt pinching at my conscience. If he wanted me to know about his mom's death, he'd have mentioned it, right? But I just had to go digging. Now I can't look him in the eye.

Julia said it's no secret, nothing to feel guilty about.

"Maddie?"

"Yes." I look up and paste a smile on my face.

His eyes narrow. "Can you come a little closer and tell me what I have on my calendar today?"

'As you always do' hangs in the air.

I do draw closer and read from the file in my hand even though I have it all in my head.

"That's your schedule for the day," I say and close the file.

"Maddie, look at me." His warm voice sears through my belly.

I look up through my lashes and he's watching me with a frown.

"Is something wrong?"

"No." I press out a fake smile.

He knows it because he only looks more worried. "Did you get home safely? Is someone bothering you?"

"No, nothing like that."

"Then, what?" His eyebrow rises. "Am I working you too much? Are you stressed?" He stands and I have the urge to take a step back, but I hold my ground.

"I'm serious. I'm fine."

He circles the desk and my stomach curls.

He's a head and shoulder taller than I am, and broader too. When a man like him advances, I should be scared.

But the only thing I feel is need, heating me from the inside out.

I clutch my file tightly and remind myself. The last time was the last.

I tilt my head to look up into his face as he stops before me.

"I'm overworking you, yes?"

I open my mouth to say no, but then he cups my cheek and runs his thumb over my lower lip. A lump forms in my throat and no words can escape.

"You stayed late last night and now you're at work early." His throat bobs, his eyes glued to where his thumb dips into my mouth.

I close my eyes and taste the pad of it. Just a little. This is not sex, it's... reminiscing.

He groans a low sound and my core clenches in response.

"I can make it better," he whispers.

I run my tongue across the thumb again.

"Can make you feel better." His voice is raspier. "What do you say, Maddie?"

My eyes split open and I take in his features. His finger slips from my mouth as he lets me speak. "How do you plan to achieve that?"

He glances at the desk. "Just sit on it for me, legs apart."

My core clenches. "Isn't that sex?" I sound breathless. "We agreed not to do that."

"It's not sex." In one smooth move, he spins me around, and backs me up to the desk.

I brace myself on his shoulders as he helps me up.

It's the opposite of what I should be doing. I should be leaving, saying no, sticking to my guns.

But his hands rub up and down my thighs and I find my legs parting, my skirt rolling up to give him access.

My head falls back as he leans in and leaves a hot kiss on my neck. "Should I?"

"We agreed not to." So why am I arching my back and pushing into his kiss?

"It's not sex, Maddie." He kisses down the center of my chest and licks my skin. "Just gonna eat you out. Give you relief."

I moan softly. I want it. But I shouldn't. Blurred lines and all that. Julia already suspects. Sure many are already gossiping about it. It's not okay.

But I want him.

"Yes," I whisper.

That one word unleashes the beast.

He yanks my skirt up and pulls down my panties. His mouth devours the swells of my breasts with wet kisses and sweet nips.

"Chance…" I whimper, pushing down on his shoulder.

He obliges and lets my breasts go.

His shoulders edge my thighs apart as he presses his lips to my center.

A long moan slips from my throat and I lift my pelvis for better access.

Chance takes it with a growl. His hands clutch my hips tight and he spreads my pussy lips open with hard licks.

I gasp, shocked by his ferocity and the need pumping through me, making me jerk up into his forceful kisses.

Pleasure slices through me as his tongue licks up and down my slit, then spears inside me. I grip his hair, holding him steady as I rock into his face.

"Yes," he says raggedly. His hands drift to my ass and he holds me open, eating me like he's a caveman with his first cut of meat in weeks.

My back hits the desk and my moans skyrocket.

Chance thumbs apart my pussy lips and then the flat of his tongue sweeps over my clit.

My lower back arches and a gasp leaves me. He goes over it, again and again, until I'm a panting, pleading mess.

"Please, Chance."

I'm not certain what I'm asking for, but I know it's only him that can give it to me.

His mouth leaves my center and alarm shoots through me.

Is he stopping?

I try to sit up but he pushes me back down and then my legs are coming up.

"What?" I say, breathless.

Chance holds my legs and dives back in.

This position, where I have no say, as he eats me, sends my body shaking.

Anyone can walk through the door and see us, see my boss treating me like a snack.

I start to tremble. "Chance, I think... I'm..."

He finds my clit and circles it, again and again. Then he spears two fingers into my pussy, stretching me out.

My orgasm hits me like a freight train. I explode into a million pleasured pieces as he rides out my orgasm with long licks and his spearing fingers.

Only when I sink back onto the desk does he let up. He kisses my inner thighs, then pulls my panties back up.

Then he leans over me. There's a smile in his eyes. "Have lunch with me."

"Is lunch code for something?" I'm still breathing heavily.

He smirks. "Yes, code for eating real food." Then his tongue sweeps over his still-wet lower lip and I think I'll take whatever lunch is, food or not.

Chapter Thirteen

Chance

The restaurant I chose to have lunch with Maddie has an ocean view and more importantly, is far from the Island's business district, meaning it won't be crowded.

I'm right.

The lunch crowd is sparse. We claim a table by the window where Maddie can watch the waves slap the beach before pulling back.

Her gaze is fixed on it, a small smile playing on her lips.

It's the perfect opportunity to watch her.

Her hand is braced under her chin, her hair floating around her as the cool salty air blows around us.

She sees something that makes her frown and purses her lips. That small pout is enough to make my heart skip a little faster and my throat closes up.

I don't understand my reaction to her. And now's not the time to try to.

This morning, I wasn't doing much thinking when I went down on her and then asked her to have lunch with me.

Maddie's not just anyone I can forget. So I definitely shouldn't be looking for more opportunities for us to be alone together.

I imagined it would be one and done with her, finishing what we started in the garden. But now it's getting to be more and I'm not sure how to deal with it.

She turns, a bright smile on her lips. "This is so lovely." She waves around us. "Seems cultural in a way."

She's referring to decor. Wooden beams make up the roof and the walls. Rustic tables and chairs cover the sitting area and green palms hang overhead. Combined with the sound and smell of the sea, it gave a feel of the outdoors but with comfort.

"How often do you come here?"

The last time I did was two years ago. "Not often."

"Huh." She looks everywhere but at me. "Because it's not your kind of place?"

Do I have a kind of place? That'd be my office. It's quiet and I can do the most work there. But I'm certain that's not what she's asking.

"No, because I've had no reason to until now."

Her lip quirks and her gaze falls to the smooth table.

Is she shy?

Before I can ask about that, she picks up the menu and starts discussing options. Glad there's something to do aside from staring at her and getting lost in my head, we go over what we'd like.

A waiter comes over and takes our orders. A seafood pasta for her, and a pork soup and potato salad for me.

We're served a coconut cocktail while we wait.

"It's weird how the beach is so quiet." She gazes out the window as a couple walks past. "The public beaches we have back home are stuffed full of people. I'd rather stay home in the summer."

I frown. I've never been one to idle away time on the beach but there were fun days when I was young. My brothers and I had fun swimming, surfing, and playing on the sand. "That's sad."

She shrugs. "It's not bad. We made the most of it. I had my family with me and we had fun."

"And your family is?"

"My mom and dad and me."

"You're an only child?"

"Uh-huh." She sips from her glass.

"Did you ever miss not having more siblings?"

She rolls her eyes up thoughtfully. "No, not really. I've been friends with Nat since we were teenagers. It's like I've always had a sister."

A smile pulls at my lips. "I've never had a sister. Well, there's Lucy but she's..."

"One of the boys?"

"Yeah."

Maddie smiles. "I saw her almost floor Baxter."

"And she would have if there wasn't dinner before us."

Her smile grows. "I don't know what it means to have a brother, either."

"My brothers can—" *be yours?* I bite my tongue. Where did that thought come from? "—can be buttheads. You're not missing out."

"Especially Baxter, right?"

I recognize the teasing twinkle in her eyes. But I hate that she finds anything to do with Baxter funny at all.

"He's a punk."

She throws her head back with a laugh. "You're very big brother-ish."

"And how's that?" I raise an eyebrow.

"You boss them around a lot, don't you?"

"I don't."

"Oh, yeah, you do." She leans in, her smile conspiratorial. "You can tell me, I won't judge."

My lip twitches. "I'm not like that. We're all grownups, we mind our business."

"Except Baxter?"

I frown. "Why are you bringing him up?"

"Because you take on this look anytime I do." She pinches her forehead together and presses her lips into a thin line.

I turn away so she doesn't see my smile. "I've never done that."

"I can start a video and when I say Baxter— Wait, look, you just did it!" She laughs.

I shake my head and drain my glass. "I didn't do anything."

"You did. Look, I'll show you." She starts to take out her phone but the waiter shows up just then, bringing our lunches. "Saved by the meal."

"You had nothing."

"Oh?" Her brow goes up, her eyes challenging. "You know what? I'm going to do it when you least expect it."

"Surprise me."

She has a game face on. "I will."

The waiter leaves and she grins at the wide plate before her. "Smells delicious."

"It does." I pick up my fork. "Dig in?"

She already forks her meal into her mouth. Her eyes are wide at me. "I didn't know I had to wait."

I chuckle. "You don't have to. Go on."

With a happy groan, she continues eating.

I usually don't have lunch, preferring to close myself in my office and do more work. So it's awkward pretending I want to eat. The food is delicious, but I don't have much of an appetite for it.

The only thing I seem to have an appetite for is watching and listening to Maddie.

She's a ball of energy, talking about the flavors in the dish, the places she's been, and what she's had there.

"By far the Island has the tastiest dishes I've had. And those cute little cakes at the Resort. Nice!"

I don't interrupt. Her animated features keep me spellbound. Only when she drops her fork do I glance at my watch.

It's already five minutes past the time I planned to stay.

"Hey, aren't you eating?" Maddie points to my half-full plate.

"I am. Lunch isn't my thing."

"Oh." Maddie bites her lower lip. "Then why did you ask us to have lunch if you weren't hungry?"

"It's still part of the plan to make you less stressed since I'm a good boss."

Her face reddens and she looks away. She's probably replaying earlier today when she writhed on my desk, rubbing her sweet pussy all over my face.

I'm suddenly craving *that* over pork.

"Do you want dessert?"

Her eyes flash at me, the redness in her cheeks spreading down to her chest.

"A real dessert," I clarify.

"Oh, yes." She laughs. "I thought you meant the other kind." She facepalms, her shoulders trembling with laughter. "Don't know why my mind went there."

"Would you say yes to that kind of dessert, though?"

"No," she says, but there's a slight shake in her voice. "We're not doing that, remember?"

I grin. "Of course."

Her eyes narrow but she lets it go.

The waiter clears our plates and brings her a coconut cake and pineapple iced tea.

Maddie makes quick work of it. Too quick.

"Do you want anything else?" I ask.

"What?" She smiles. "No. I'm stuffed." She taps her belly.

"Sure?" If she's no longer eating, there's no reason for us to keep staying here. And that means we have to get back to work and I won't get to hear her laughter or her jokes or look into her eyes for minutes uninterrupted.

"Yes," she stresses. "Plus, this is the longest lunch ever. I have work to get back to."

"And what if I say you don't have to work today?"

"I'll tell you that I'll still need to complete it tonight or worse, tomorrow."

"Yeah, that's true."

"Can we go now?"

I refuse to think that's because she's bored of me. Like me, Maddie's work ethic is top-notch. So much so she challenges me to do better.

She probably just wants to get back to that and I'm not going to deny her.

After I settle the bill, we head out. We're at the entrance when I spot Baxter coming in.

Fuck.

I place my hand on Maddie's lower back, set to steer her away, but Baxter spots us.

"Miss Lowe and my favorite brother." His grin grows wide as he stops before us and holds out his arms.

She glances at me and smiles right before she tucks herself in them for a brief second.

I know she's proving that Baxter's presence annoys me. But what she doesn't know is that it's because he wants her. And I won't let him have her.

"Baxter." I ignore the bro hug he tries to initiate. "What are you doing here?"

"Coming in from tennis practice." He waves his hand to his running shoes paired with jersey shorts and a shirt that molds to his biceps. "And what are you two up to?"

"Having lunch. With my girlfriend."

"Huh." He looks between us, then asks Maddie, "How was lunch?"

"Delicious. You're going to enjoy it."

"Oh, I know. I come here a lot." He looks at me like *'you don't, why now?'*

I won't dignify that look with a response. I wouldn't have brought Maddie if I knew there was a likelihood that we would run into each other.

"Wait, so after tennis and lunch you'll return to the office?" Maddie asks.

He laughs. "No. I don't roll the way Chance does. The world is my oyster." He splays his hands.

"Shut your sweaty pits." To Maddie, I say, "He takes possible investors on fun little dates and convinces them to invest with us."

"Oh." She nods.

"Yep." Baxter winks. "And because I'm not petty I won't take offense to Chance belittling my very serious, very important job."

"I'm sure he didn't mean that." She turns to me, her face solemn.

"He did," Baxter says.

"I did," I concur.

Before she can delve more into our weird dynamic, an older couple comes up to stand next to Baxter.

"Mr. and Mrs. Kelly, this is my brother, CEO Chance Easton, and his assistant, Maddie Lowe."

Maddie and I exchange handshakes with the Kellys.

"She's my girlfriend, too," I add.

Mrs. Kelly smiles. "You two look wonderful, dear."

"And we'll need to sit with you soon, Mr. Easton," Mr. Kelly says.

"Chance, please."

He nods. "Right now, we're hungry."

"Aye," his wife agrees. "We've worked up an appetite playing tennis."

"They are excellent players." Baxter smiles. "I couldn't keep up."

The couple smiles proudly before drifting away.

If only they knew Baxter probably held back to keep them happy.

"What about you, Maddie? Do you play?"

Why is he talking to her? "She—"

"Yes," she says.

"—does?" I look down at her.

"You didn't know that?" Baxter smirks. "What a boyfriend."

"I didn't tell him," Maddie says.

Wait, is she defending me? My chest fills up with a feeling I can't name.

"We should play sometime," Baxter says, snapping me back to the moment. "Maybe Friday?"

"We're busy on Friday," I cut in before he can force Maddie to commit.

"We are?"

"With work."

"I'm talking evening." Baxter's smile is smug.

"We are busy then too."

"Oh, come on," he drawls.

"Really? I didn't know that." Maddie frowns at me.

"I didn't tell you. But we're—" Think. *Think.* "We're going on a date." I keep my gaze firmly on Baxter.

"Oh," is all Maddie says.

Baxter's eyes narrow. "Is that so?"

"It is. So she can't go playing tennis with you."

His smile is broad. "Too bad, then. Enjoy your date." He nods toward the Kellys. "I'll rejoin my tennis buddies."

I watch him saunter off, knowing I have to explain to Maddie about this sudden date. But glad nonetheless that Baxter doesn't get to spend any time with her.

Chapter Fourteen

Maddie

I'm pacing my living room. Pacing.

I stop as I feel a trickle down my cheek. I wipe and my fingers come away wet. I'm working up a sweat.

No, no, no.

Quickly, I grab a towel and dab my face, then fight the urge to walk off my nervous energy.

There's no reason I should be nervous. It's only a date with my boss I've been seeing all day. But I am.

My stomach's coiling and my heart's thumping faster.

I glare at the clock, willing it to become seven p.m. so I can be put out of my misery.

Why do I feel so weird?

Chance and I shared that fun lunch a couple of days ago. I wasn't nervous about that. Why now?

I walk over to the room and stand before the floor-length mirror. The matte green evening gown hugs my skin like a loving caress, but is free enough that I can move easily. The emerald studs in my ear complement the simple look. As does my hair packed up and away from my face in a cute little updo.

There. I look... like I'm about to go on a real date with someone I actually like.

And I'm feeling a rush of nerves like it.

I drop into the bed and recite the words.

"This means nothing. It's only a date."

The grind of car tires on asphalt brings my head up. The engine shuts off and a door bangs.

He's here.

Swallowing down my nerves, I grab my purse and head to the front door. A soft knock slips through right before I open it.

My... world.

He's in a warm brown short-sleeved button-down, paired with darker slacks and boots.

I'm sure my mouth is open and my eyes are wide. But I can't stop.

All my nerves have disappeared, leaving a tremor that rushes through me all brought about by the sight of him.

I meet his eyes and my knees grow weak.

His deep blue gaze is smoky as it glides over me.

I'm torn between running away from the energy sizzling between us and skipping into his arms, begging him to take me.

Before I can do either very stupid things, he breaks the silence.

"You look amazing." It's a whisper, a rumble.

My heart stutters. "And so do you."

His lips quirk. "You ready?"

I nod, unable to speak. He reaches out a hand and I place my palm in it.

Our eyes meet and I know he feels it too.

The electricity sizzling between us.

I only hope I can get through tonight without doing something stupid.

On the ride to the restaurant, I remind myself it's only a date. Over and over.

"What date?" Chance asks as he turns into the parking lot.

"Hmm?" My gaze whips to him. Shit. I've been muttering out loud. "No date. It's nothing."

He sticks next to me as we proceed into the fancy restaurant. Everything is coated in a warm glow, and elegantly dressed patrons chat across primly decorated tables. It's unlike the rustic restaurant we visited for lunch, but nice nonetheless. Maybe it's not the place but the man.

I only realize I've been staring at his profile when his gaze drops to me.

I can't look away.

He holds my eyes for a long second. Then smiles. "Come on."

Hand on my lower back, he directs us to a table and pulls out my chair.

He takes his seat opposite me and immediately picks up his menu, obstructing my view.

I put a finger on top of it and pull it down. "What are you doing?"

"Choosing what to eat?"

"Is that what you do on dates, *boyfriend?*"

He opens his mouth but no words come out. "What am I to do?"

"Talk to me, I guess. Have you ever been on a date before?"

"You usually do most of the talking. For some reason, you're quiet tonight and…"

I frown. "And?"

"I don't know." He shrugs, and promptly shields his face again.

Wait, what? Is he nervous and unsure? *THE* Chance Easton?

I start to laugh and press my hand to my lips to stifle the sound.

He drops his menu. "What are you doing?"

"You're cute when you're nervous."

"I'm not nervous." He looks away.

His jaw twitches with held-back laughter.

"You are. And I am too."

He looks back at me warily.

"And that's okay," I say quietly. "I'm on a date with my boss. That's daunting."

"Boyfriend."

"Fake boyfriend," I amend.

He smiles.

"We can just be nervous together." I shrug. Cheesy as fuck but it works.

Chance is more relaxed and my heart's not running a thousand miles a minute any longer.

We discuss the menu and place our orders. Then Chance tells me about his childhood on Magic Island.

"I've visited other places, but I always come home. There's everything here," he says, his eyes turning dreamy. "There's family, the beaches, the woods..."

"And your employees to boss around?"

He laughs. "Yes, exactly. Can't leave them to roam free, can I?"

I smile. "Certainly not."

We chat about everything and nothing as we tuck in our meals. When we're finishing up our desserts, I can't believe the time has gone so fast.

I don't want it to end.

It's only a date.

But the way he smiles across the table and leans forward. His eyes are on me like I'm the only person that exists in his world. It's making my pulse race with something other than just wanting us between the sheets together.

I want... more.

Fuck. No, I can't think that.

We exit the restaurant and get into the car. It's a quiet drive back to the Resort. I alternate between looking at Chance and out the window.

He stops in front of the villa and gets out as I do. He waits for me to come around and we start up the walkway together.

He walks in measured steps as if he doesn't want the night to be over.

Or is that my wishful thinking?

We climb up the porch steps and the night is set to be over. We face each other.

"We're here," I sing, trying to smile but failing woefully.

"Yeah, we are." There's no smile on his face. Just the overhead lamp highlighting his features. He looks tense. Why? I'm not sure.

"Hmm." I nod. "So, this is goodnight?"

Why am I asking? Of course, it is.

His brow goes up but he doesn't reply. Instead, his eyes drop to my lips. I lick them instinctively and his chest heaves.

I swallow, looking at his lips too now, wanting him.

I shouldn't.

He closes the gap between us suddenly, his lips claiming mine. The breath leaves my lungs as his body presses into mine and his arms wrap around me, pulling me against him.

I open my mouth to receive his kiss and his tongue dives in.

I'm panting, trying to hold on. Just as I let my purse go, he spins us so my back meets the wall. I grab his neck and pull him down, kissing him more deeply.

He groans, hands caressing down to my ass and squeezing. His grip hardens and he thrusts.

My eyes split wide and I meet his heated gaze. He's hard steel, poking against my lower belly. I gasp, my core clenching with need.

Damn our earlier agreement, I want him to fuck me. Hard.

"I'll get the door," I say.

He steps back, giving me room to grab my purse where I tossed it.

I pick it up and run my fingers through it. There's my phone, lipstick, kerchief... where's the key? "A moment." I back him and search through it more thoroughly.

Oh, no. Can't find it.

We're both still breathing heavily, but it's growing quieter as my search for the key stretches on.

"What's wrong?" Chance's voice is hoarse with need.

A shiver rushes through me. I want him. "Can't find the damn key."

"Let me help." He takes the purse and takes everything out. "It's not here."

"But I locked the door and put the key in it." I look around. "Maybe it fell out when I dropped the purse."

"Plausible." He notes. "No zipper."

Just a clasp. Fuck.

"Where did the purse fall?" He crouches.

"There." I point to a spot and step aside as he starts to search.

I take out my phone and help with a flashlight. It takes a lot of looking before we spot it.

The light winks off the key where it fell between the flowers.

"Got it!" Chance rises with a grin.

I smile back. "Thank you."

He drops it in my hand and I insert it. I turn the key and the door unlocks.

I glance back at Chance. He's standing with his hands in his pockets, his eyes solemn. I don't need to ask, I know he's not coming in.

Searching for the key brought on a reality check. Everything from the kiss to the nearly letting him in was breaking our agreement.

Still, I'm tempted.

"Would you—"

"Goodn—"

We say at the same time.

"You go first," I concede.

A smile plays on his lips. "Goodnight, right?"

He's the smarter one of us two. I was about to invite him in for coffee.

And I'm the one who said no sex.

"Yeah, sure."

He nods. "See you on Monday, Maddie."

He turns and heads down the walkway. He gets into his car and I expect him to drive off, but he looks back at me.

Oh, he's waiting for me to go in.

Of course. I push the door open and enter.

Seconds later, I hear the start of an engine.

Sighing, I drop onto my couch, staring up at the ceiling.

The feverish need pulsing through me has become a low thrum. I can still feel Chance's lips, his searing touch, and his heated gaze.

I groan. If I didn't throw the purse and lost the key, we would have been on my bed now. Or maybe we wouldn't have made it that far. Either way, I'll be a very happy woman who'd have regrets in the morning, but happy nonetheless.

Now, I won't have regrets but I'm left aching.

Shutting my eyes, I push my hands down to my center. Maybe I can just fix this.

A knock at the door has me sitting up.

Is he back? Did he change his mind?

Excitement pulses through my body.

I hop to my feet.

The knock sounds again, more urgent.

He must be eager.

I quickly fix my hair and straighten my dress, then I pull the door open.

The man before me is not Chance. He's in all black with a mask covering his face. A scream tears from my throat and I push the door.

A foot appears between the door and the frame. The man reaches a hand in to grab me and I scoot out of the way.

"Open the fucking door!" he yells.

"No!" I push back but he's gaining on me. He's stronger and I can't keep him out for long.

Except... I stare down at that foot. It's booted but with enough force I can do some damage.

I release my hold on the door for a split second then push back with all my strength. The door slams against the foot and the man howls.

The force pushing back against me from his end disappears and I'm able to close the door. With my heart racing and breath heaving, I shut the door and clip all the locks in place.

I rush to find my phone and dial Chance's number. "Please, pick up."

I balance the phone between my shoulder and ear, rushing through the house and making sure all the windows are locked.

"Maddie?" Chance answers, finally.

"Someone was at my door."

"What?"

"Someone came to my door. I thought it was you and I opened and they tried to get me and I fought back but I don't know what to do. What if they come back?" I'm shaking, my voice is shaking.

But Chance sounds calm. Too calm. "Stay away from the door, Maddie. Can you hear me?"

"Yes, yes."

"Don't open for anyone until you hear my voice. Are all your windows locked?"

"Yes."

"Good girl. I'll be there in a minute."

A minute feels like an eternity as I wait for Chance to show up. All the terrible what-ifs leave me trembling.

"Maddie!"

My body jerks.

"Maddie, it's me. Chance. Open up."

I rush to the door and pull it open. He's there indeed.

Relief swoops through me and I rush into his open arms.

"You're alright." He holds me close, patting my hair. "I'm here, okay?"

My trembling ebbs and I look up to meet his eyes. "I'm so scared. What am I going to do?"

"We can't think of that right now. For tonight, you're coming with me, okay? Go get your things."

I nod quickly and go back inside, glad I don't have to stay here.

Chapter Fifteen

Chance

The doorbell rings. I know it's Baxter. I take my time, sipping my coffee as casually as I can. It goes off again. The only reason I go to get it is because Maddie's asleep upstairs and after the night she's had, she needs all the rest she can get.

Baxter's looking irritatingly sunny in his shorts and t-shirt.

"Fuck you," I say, stepping aside to let him through.

"I haven't even said a word."

I ignore him and head back to the kitchen. My mug is nearly empty so I start another pot.

"Bad night, huh?" Baxter slides onto a stool around the kitchen island.

"What do you want?" I bite out.

"Dude, I'm here every Saturday. Why so salty this morning?"

"You just seem happier than usual." I eye him.

"And you seem grumpy as always. Now if you get laid, I assure you, it will be better for us all."

"Stop. You're just thrilled she's here."

He scoffs. "You insecure, little shit. You know I don't see Maddie that way. When are you going to tell her you want her for real?"

"What do you mean?" I take my seat and chug down the remaining coffee. It's black the way I like it. Great at helping me get my head together, but it's not working today. Especially with Baxter sitting across from me, bothering me with his senseless theories.

"Ask her to be your girlfriend."

"She is my girlfriend."

"Yeah, right." Baxter grins. "We both know she's not. You only asked her to fake it so I don't charm her into falling in love with me, yes?"

I hate how dead on the money he is. Smart bastard. "Who else knows?"

"No one does. And they don't have to find out. Make it real and stop torturing yourself."

I eyeball him. "I'm good. But thanks for the advice, love guru."

"That's what the ladies call me." He smirks.

I'm tempted to throw my coffee at him. Too bad the mug is empty.

"Look." Baxter sits forward. "You're not doing yourself or her any favors by pretending you don't want her."

"I don't—" I can't say the word. It'll be a big ass lie and Baxter would see through it. He already has.

I climb off the stool and go to pour myself a fresh cup of coffee. He's silent which is unusual but I know he's giving me room to say my peace.

I sigh and brace my hands on the counter. "It's not that simple. She's leaving in a week and I don't know how it's supposed to work. I've kept her from her life long enough."

"Have you asked her, though? Given her a choice or are you just choosing for her?"

His words hit me and I pause. I never considered that. I just assumed she'd leave and we'd be over.

But she repeated it too. I'd be dumb not to listen. She wants to keep the lines between us clear. No matter how much she wants me, she wants nothing more than these three weeks have to offer.

I pour myself a full cup and burn my throat drinking the steaming liquid. "She doesn't want it." I drop into the chair and face Baxter.

"And you know that, how?" He folds his arms.

"She has said it."

"In what context?"

I refuse to dissect that. If I do, I'll give myself false hope. And want something I shouldn't. Something I can never have.

Because it's all my fault.

I shut down that thought. "Are you a therapist now?" I glare at him. "Mind your business."

He shrugs, unfazed by my hostility. "I don't know, man. Sometimes, I wonder if you actually need one."

I climb off the stool and Baxter climbs off his, hands out. He circles the island as I advance toward him. "Calm down, big guy. I'm just throwing options out there. Seeing if a dart hits the bullseye. That's all."

I stop by my coffee and take another drink, dropping back into my stool. My sigh is heavy. "I have to keep her safe and make sure she gets home like we agreed, that's all."

I don't need to look at my brother to know he's no longer smiling.

"You need to tell her, idiot. Try to keep her."

"It's only a fucking week left!" I bite out.

"Well, congrats. Enjoy your last week of the little happiness you've had in ages."

I growl and finish off my coffee. I hate that he's right. I hate that there's nothing I can do about it.

The soft patter of footsteps makes me sit straighter. Landon is closed off in the study, his head buried in his work. So that's not him.

That's her.

Baxter realizes it at the same time I do. He smiles just as she rounds the corner.

"Miss Lowe, fancy seeing you on a Saturday morning."

She spares him a smile, then looks between both of us. "I had a not-so-good night."

"I heard. I'm sorry about that."

"No, I'm sorry for intruding." She looks my way, her gaze solemn.

I don't want her to feel that way. She's always welcome here. Despite the night, I slept well knowing she was down the hall and within reach if she needed me.

Obviously, she didn't.

"Coffee?" I ask.

"Yes, thank you." She takes the stool beside Baxter.

I don't mind turning my back to them as I prepare her coffee. He won't try to woo her. Our conversation this morning let me know that much.

I've just poured her coffee when I realize I have no idea how she likes it. So I place the mug with creamer and sugar before her.

"Oh, babe." She forces cheer into her tone. "You know I like my coffee one part cream with two cubes of sugar."

She's putting on a show for Baxter. If only she knew.

But I store her preferences anyway. I can't help it.

It's probably useless information now that she's leaving in a week. But my brain has a special section for Maddie. I know her favorite everything. The things she won't touch with a ten-foot pole. And the maybes in her book.

I'm staring at her sip from her mug when my gaze shifts. I find Baxter watching me, an accusation in his gaze.

I glare back. Just because he knows I'm interested in Maddie doesn't mean he can force my hand.

"Hey, Maddie," Baxter says.

"Hmm?" She turns his way, her eyes brighter than when she first came downstairs.

"What do you think about a game of tennis since we're both here?"

She glances at me. "That sounds like fun."

Baxter eyes me. "What do you think about that, brother?"

I shrug. "Enjoy your game."

His brows lift with surprise. He probably thought I'd throw a fit and he'd prove something.

I'm not worried about him anymore.

"Fine." He climbs off the stool. "I'll get the bats and balls."

He's gone, leaving Maddie and me alone.

She looks over the rim of her mug and meets my eyes. "I'm sorry."

"Fuck, Maddie."

I round the island and pull her into my arms.

Her slender arms go around my waist, holding on tight.

"It's not your fault. You shouldn't be sorry."

"But I'm causing you so much trouble." She pulls back to look at my face. "Shouldn't I just go back to the city?"

"No," I say a little too firmly that her brows furrow. I smoothen that frown with a rub of my thumb. "No. You'll stay and complete your time as you want, okay? No one will run you off my island. I won't let them."

Her eyes soften.

"You want to stay the week, right?" If she says no, I'll let her leave but I probably won't recover from the hurt.

"Of course," she breathes.

I smile, cup her face, and plant a kiss on her forehead.

She tilts her head back as if offering her lips. It's a gift I'm about to take when Baxter returns.

"I've got them." His eyes fall on us and he grins, starting to turn away. "I can just wait."

"Do that," I say.

"No, I'm ready." Maddie slips out of my arms and off the stool.

She meets up with Baxter and they head to the court that's off to the side of the property.

I climb up to the balcony and look down at them. They make an interesting pair. It looks like she won't get in a hit. Baxter's a huge fellow with arm strength that matches mine. I almost want to ask him to take it easy on her.

When the first five minutes are over, I'm happy I didn't intrude. Maddie's nimble on her feet, skipping across the court and catching all of Baxter's hits. They go back and forth until one of them caves, but it's tense and they're evenly matched.

Maddie scores a hit and cheers, hands over her head. "Yes!" She spins around and grins at me.

I can't help my smile. I throw her a salute and she returns it.

Then she's taunting Baxter, asking him to bring it on.

As she holds him off, I take out my phone and call the head of the security team I assigned to watch Maddie.

"Found him yet?" I know more than one person is likely involved in the threats against Maddie. But one was bold enough to come close. That one, I need to set an example with.

"Not yet," the voice at the other end replies. "We've combed the entire area around the Resort and close by. Nothing."

I sigh, pinching my forehead. "What do you mean nothing? You were meant to be watching her last night. If she didn't fight back, anything could have happened."

My chest hurts just thinking about it.

"We've doubled the security to watch her. Last night won't repeat itself."

"Only doubled?"

"Triple," he says quickly. "We will triple it. We've also made sure all the security cameras around the Resort are working well.

And we've added more cameras to the blind spots we found. Nothing will get by us again."

"You have to promise me that," I bite out. "If not, it's over for you and your team."

"I swear it, Mr. Easton."

"Good." I disconnect the call, eyes focused on the game once more.

Baxter takes this round and yells his victory. Maddie makes a stink face at him.

She's set to serve again.

"Go, Maddie!" I shout.

Baxter glares at me. "Come on. I'm winning."

"Not for long," I return.

Maddie laughs at Baxter's irritation and they go another round.

My phone beeps. I scroll through the email. It's from the security team giving a detailed explanation about their strategy to keep Maddie safe at the Resort. It could as well be a president they're protecting with all the resources they're using up.

I don't care how far they have to go. As long as she's safe.

I look to see her. She has a big smile on, her face glowing beneath the morning sun. She's radiant, almost as if last night didn't happen. So brave to fight off an intruder and call me immediately after in those circumstances. I'll do all I can to keep her safe.

I considered keeping her here in my home. I won't let her out of my sight and no one will get close enough to hurt her.

But I have to keep my end of the bargain. She'll retain her home at the Resort as we agreed to in the first place.

I'm honorable enough to give her that much even though I want different.

Maddie wins this round and dances. Baxter doesn't take it and starts another round. He wins it.

Maddie collapses to the floor, heaving. "Can we take a break?"

My brother laughs. "Sure thing." He waves me over. "Come on, big guy. Come show us what you've got."

Maddie's gaze whips to me, interest stirring in her eyes.

I take up Baxter's challenge if only to impress her, and prove I can beat them both together at the same time.

Chapter Sixteen

Maddie

"Hello?" I say into the phone balanced between my ear and shoulder.

I took the call before I saw the caller ID. Doesn't matter though. It won't be long. I've got work to catch up on. Anyone calling at nine a.m. on a Monday would understand.

"Meet me in the parking lot."

I sit up. "Chance?"

"Yes. Don't tell me you don't have my number saved."

"I do."

"Good. Be out in five minutes."

I'm about to explain what I'm working on when the call ends. Blowing out a breath, I roll my eyes.

Why the parking lot? Can't we meet in his office? But he's the boss and I can't have too many questions.

Since no one's in the conference room, I leave my laptop and files with Julia on my way down. Hopefully, this won't take long and I can come back to wrap up my tasks.

Strangely, there are no meetings for today. They've all been canceled, Julia said when I asked earlier. She had no clue why or who did that.

I thought I'd have the whole morning to do in-office work, but nope.

I step out through the doors and walk across the concrete floor to the parking lot. I spot Chance's car and head over there.

He's leaning against the side, his face glued to his phone. His tall frame is wrapped up nicely in a casual light brown suit with dark brown shoes to match.

My insides swim with need, as it always does when I set eyes on him.

I almost agree with Nat's rant last night when I called to tell her about the intruder.

"You slept down the hall from him and didn't even get a cuddle? Are you crazy?"

"Nat, I was frightened."

"All the more reason why you should have asked him to stay with you and—"

"We're not sleeping together, remember?"

"You should have. How romantic would it have been?"

Then I had to explain why we couldn't be romantic.

Now, though, I'm considering it. He was nothing but sweet when he took me from the villa to his home. Then he drove me back after assuring me everything was safe and stayed until I promised I'd be fine.

I'm only worried because I'm not imagining just sex. I'm imagining the stuff that comes after, the things that only lovers do. Like cuddles, cozying up on a couch together to watch a movie, and having regular dates.

"I'm here," I say a little too loudly to announce my presence and shut down those thoughts swirling through my head.

He looks up and his eyes soften.

They always seem to do that when they fall on me. Does that mean... nope, no!

"Get in."

I pause. What?

"Into the car," he says after a beat.

One moment I'm swooning and the next he's ordering me about. So bossy.

I round the car and get in. He enters after me and starts the car.

"What's happening?" I frown. "Where are we going?"

"You'll see."

Um, what?

His phone starts to ring. Without looking at it, Chance presses the off button, then tosses it in the back.

What is going on? I don't ask, though. I'm certain he'll give another non-answer.

Maybe we're attending a meeting that just came up. But he didn't ask me to bring my laptop. How will I take notes? Or make references?

I eye his profile and he's a picture of control, as always. Nothing slips by him. If he wanted me to bring my laptop, he'd have stated it.

I sit back and try to relax, but I'm not very successful. We don't go to another company building or a hall, instead, we're driving out of the business district.

I hold my tongue, curiosity winning over confusion.

Chance turns off the main highway into a narrower street. The road is winding and the air is cooler, more salty. Around us, the dense trees thin, giving way to palm trees.

It doesn't take long to hear the churning of the ocean. I glance at Chance, my brows furrowed. Maybe he forgot the way to where we're supposed to go.

But he drives confidently and pulls up at the beach, then the car stops.

I look at him until he turns to me. His brow goes up in a silent question.

"What are we doing here?"

"What do you mean? We're here to have fun at the beach. You looked like you wanted to come the other day."

My jaw drops. "You remember that?"

"Don't make it a thing." He looks away and exits the car.

I follow suit, still gaping. I spare the ocean a wide-eyed look before turning to the man looking off into the distance.

"Chance, this is sweet." It's hard to walk with my shoes in the sand but I manage to reach him.

He looks down at me, a line between his brows as if he disapproves that I called his gesture sweet.

"But I'm not dressed for the beach." I point to my gown and shoes. "And neither are you."

He takes off his jacket and shoes and tosses them in the car. "You can just take off the shoes."

"And ruin my dress?"

His gaze slides over me. "I'll get you another."

"Chance, you don't—"

I'm whisked off my feet before I can finish that thought.

He throws me over his shoulder. His hand clamps down on my legs and my hands and torso hang down his back.

A scream tears from my throat. "What are you doing?"

He takes off my shoes and then we're moving.

"Chance!" I slap his back. "Put me down."

His chest rumbles with laughter but he doesn't stop.

I only understand his plan when I hear the waves very close.

"No, don't you dare." I grab the fabric of his shirt tight. "Don't throw me down. Don't—"

He throws me.

I'm screaming my throat raw and holding him so firmly that we go down together. The water instantly swallows us and then recedes.

It's refreshing, but I'm mad. I face him, fury battering my chest. "What did you do that for?"

He's laughing, eyes squinted up to the sun. He's soaked from his head to his bare toes. He swipes away the hair plastered to his forehead and looks at me with bright eyes.

"You have to admit. That was a little funny."

"It's not!" I hop to my feet. "Look at my dress."

His eyes darken. "Suits you."

I look down to see that it's molded to my frame. My cheeks turn hot. "It's stained and sandy."

"A swim will make it clean." He stands and starts to come my way.

I know his intent and I yelp, racing in the opposite direction. "No!"

His hands wrap around my waist and we're one with waves again. This time, I come up laughing. Fuck his crazy tactics, but the diving is fun.

"Okay, okay. I'm clean now." I rise and back away.

"Are you?" He stands.

"Mm-hmm." I nod, glancing behind him at the waves rushing toward us.

Once they're close, I push against his chest. His eyes widen before he falls into the water.

I laugh, clapping my hands. "I got you!"

Chance has a playful frown on his face once he comes up again. "You think you did something there, huh?"

"Oh, I know I did." I take a step back as he takes one forward.

"Really?" He draws nearer.

"Yeah." I do a silly dance. "You went down like a freaking log. Should have seen you. What a—"

He rushes toward me. I swerve away just before he grabs me and his hand grazes my side.

I don't stop running, knowing he won't stop until he gets revenge. A look over my shoulder proves true. Chance is closing the gap.

I should be running for my life but I slow down, entranced by his features. He has a smile on his face, his eyes bright. He's soaking wet and looking very unlike himself. But the way he looks right now melts my heart.

He catches up to me and lifts me high. My heart is in my throat. I'd probably be flung as far as the middle of the ocean.

I close my eyes and hold my breath, bracing myself, but then I'm coming down gently.

I blink open and meet Chance's eyes as he places me down. His eyes, warm and blue as the ocean, take me in. Then he combs back my hair with his fingers.

"Why didn't you?" I ask quietly, my heartbeat stuttering in my chest.

"Because..." He cups my face gently. "A surprise is best!"

One moment I'm standing and the next I'm in the water.

"Like a log!" I hear Chance's triumphant shout.

I swim out, gasping for a breath. I don't care what happens, he's going down again. He's already running off when I come up.

"I'm going to get you," I swear.

He wears a smug grin. "You can try."

And I do. It's hard but I bring him down once more and the next we go down together.

As we swim, I peel off my clothes and then I'm in only my bra and panties. They're not as fancy as a bikini, but Chance doesn't mind. Neither do I when he's down to his briefs.

He's all hard planes and tan skin. I want to lick him.

He catches my gaze drifting to his bulge and he tuts. "My eyes are up here, Maddie."

"I wasn't looking at you!" I protest.

"Yeah, right." He ignores my next string of words and takes my hand. "Let's walk."

I'm effectively shut up as Chance's firm hand closes around mine. Our skins brush as we walk and the sun is warm on my back.

He stops at the car and reaches in, taking out a tube of sunscreen.

I eye him as he squirts it on my back and begins to rub. "You thought of this and not swimsuits?"

He doesn't reply.

I return the favor and try not to linger too long on his skin, even though I'm tempted.

Then we take a long walk under the warm sun. We get coconut drinks and meat kebabs and sit beneath an umbrella and have a pleasant meal.

Afterward, we head back. We pass by only a few people, which is a change from the noisy beaches I'm used to.

I'm beat by the time we gather up our things to head home.

"I'm so sandy." I pause at the passenger door.

Chance's car interior is too clean to mess up.

"Should I come and show you how to get into the car?" The threat in his voice is obvious.

But over the hood of the car, I see the sparkle in his eyes. He'd enjoy getting his hands on me.

"Nah, I'm good." I grin and hop in.

On our way, I start to feel itchy and can't sit still.

Chance glances over at me but says nothing.

We turn into the driveway of his home and I sit up.

"I'm not going back to the villa?"

"You need a bath," he says. "The Resort is farther."

I mutter a thank you and follow him in. I'm heading to the spare room I stayed in the last time I was here but he steers me to his bedroom.

"Better products," he says.

He's right. The bodywash and shampoo work like magic on my body. I step out of the shower feeling fresh. I grab a towel and dry off before heading back to Chance's room.

It's sparsely decorated like his office and there's not much to dig through.

I'm all dried up when I realize I don't have anything to wear since my clothes were ruined. Shrugging, I head to his closet and find a soft tee.

It falls to my thighs and smells like him, but it's better than a wet towel.

I hope he doesn't mind.

I'm heading back out when a sizzling sound followed by a delicious aroma fills the air. I bound to the kitchen faster.

I halt by the door.

Chance showered too from the look of things. His back is still damp with beads of water and his hair is combed clean.

It's one thing seeing him at the beach in briefs. And it's entirely another standing in an enclosed space with him a few feet away. A towel is strapped around his waist showing off the outline of his glutes and strong thighs making me hungry for something that's not food.

He turns and his eyes fall on me. They grow dark immediately as they sweep over my frame. I feel naked despite the shirt.

"I didn't have anything to wear so I borrowed your..." I pull at it, unable to speak.

He meets my eyes and I see that's not a problem at all. In fact, he seems to like it a lot.

Well, me too.

I move first, but he's faster.

The distance between us closes and he claims my mouth with a kiss.

Chapter Seventeen

Chance

Maddie's body fits against mine as our tongues roll together.

It's a heady mix, tasting her mouth while having barely any clothes between us. The shirt she has on is old and soft and fails to hide her beaded nipples and the softness of her breasts.

A groan tears from me and I walk her back until she's pressed against the island. She's still too low so I scoop her up and deposit her on the smooth marble surface.

Her soft *umph* does shit to me.

She's level with me now so I can kiss her neck and suck on the skin there. She writhes in one spot, moving her hips back and forth. Her fingers splay across my back and she's tugging me closer as if she wants me inside her—as deep as I can go.

My cock's a rod beneath the towel around my waist. It's dripping precum, begging to be let into her clenching hole.

I rub my hands up and down her thighs and she parts them easily.

"Please, Chance," she hums, her fingers running through my hair and pressing me down where I'm kissing her neck.

I leave the soft, sweet skin for a second. "Please, what?"

"Please..." She moans as I find the lobe of her ear and roll my tongue around it. "Please." Her hips buck and she rubs herself against my lower belly.

Her wetness sticks to my skin and forces a spurt of precum out of me.

She's so goddamn needy.

I want to give in. But I don't want her to feel the regret that would come after. She was pretty clear.

"You said no fucking." I catch those restless thighs and hold them apart, then I shift forward.

She's on my towel covered-cock in a second, her hips rolling around feverishly.

I pull back. "You said."

"I know what I said!" She squirms, frustration written on her features as her hips twist around but can't find the friction.

I need her to tell me straight. No lust haze getting in the way of her good sense.

"Have you changed your mind?"

"Please, Chance."

"No, I want to hear it."

"Let's just..." She slides off the counter. Her arms wind around my neck and her legs around my waist. She bounces on my dick, her moans loud in the otherwise quiet kitchen.

I let it go on. If precum could burn through fabric, my cock would no doubt be lodged into her tight seeking hole and fucking her senseless.

I grab her ass and help her ride me, faster, harder. She's breathless with need, her movements turning disjointed. It's a fucking struggle not to strip off and plunge into her.

But losing myself in the moment would do us no good, so I grab her hips to stop her movements, then I place her back on the island.

She fights me, but I hold steady and finally, she gives up, resting her ass against the surface but bathing my neck with long licks.

My balls tremble with the thought of that overactive tongue on my cock. Rolling around the head, down the veiny stalk, her eyes looking up at me.

I give in for a second and thrust forward, meeting her heat. It's so good I thrust again.

Maddie's hands start to descend when I catch myself.

"No." I grab her hands. "Maddie, look at me."

Her eyelids flutter open. Eyes glazed with lust slide over my face and stop at my lips. She licks hers and starts to lean in.

"No." My voice is hoarse with restrained need. I want to give in to whatever madness is pulling us together, but I need to know she's all in. "Do you want this?"

She swallows. "Yes."

"It's me fucking you, Maddie. I'll have my cock deep inside you and you won't know where you start or I end."

Her eyes sparkle with lust. "Yes."

"And you won't regret it?"

She shakes her head firmly.

"I need to hear it."

"I won't," she breathes.

I smile. "Say it."

A line forms between her brows before she gets it. "I won't regret you fucking me, Chance."

My cock surges to life, straining against the towel.

"I mean it." She scooches forward and places her hands on my chest. "I want you deep inside me. So deep it hurts. I want the hurt. It'll feel so good coming from you."

"Maddie." I drop my gaze because I'm barely able to maintain control with the words she's saying.

"Fuck me, Chance," she says with a small whimper. "Give it to me so good."

I snatch her off the island and then I'm heading to the bedroom. She clings to me, letting me feel all of her. I can't get there fast enough.

Once I have the door shut behind me, I slow down, placing her on the bed. She falls back against the pillows, splayed open before me.

Her eyes are closed and her body thrums with anticipation.

I need to be inside her now, but I also want the moment to last. It's always been rushed between us—in the garden, the office, but for the first time, I have her in my bed.

She blinks open and meets my eyes.

"Take it off. I want to see all of you."

She sits up and tugs the shirt off. A groan falls from my throat. Her skin is smooth porcelain. I'm afraid I'll mar it if I touch her.

She settles back on the pillows, her hands behind her head and her thighs lined up.

"Your turn," she says.

With a single tug, the towel is off. My cock bounces free, straining toward her, eager to get into the center of her thighs.

Her lips part and she licks the bottom one.

I grab my cock and resist the need to grunt. I stroke up and down, keeping my eyes on her. With every tug on the head, her chest heaves faster. I run my thumb down the slit and she gasps, then swallows.

"Want to suck on it?"

She nods.

I straddle her body and position my cock over her lips. "You'll tell me if it's too much?"

Another nod, and then she pushes off my hands and replaces them with hers. Her hands around my cock pull a groan from me. Before I can settle into that feeling, her hot mouth closes around me.

"Fuck, Maddie." I buck into her, catch myself and try to pull back.

But she grasps me hard and pulls me deeper.

"Maddie—" I grunt, not wanting to but unable to resist thrusting just a little.

The way she's taking it, so hungry for cock, it's getting to my head, killing my resolve to take it slow.

I meet the back of her throat. I swear to the ceiling, holding back the need to erupt. She's going to pull back now and give me relief.

But her throat muscles unclench, and then I'm going deeper.

I look down, shocked to see my cock touch base in her mouth. Her eyes are wide and excited and she writhes beneath me.

Her palms come up to my glutes and she squeezes rhythmically. Asking me to fuck her throat?

Jesus.

I do so. Just little thrusts. Her eyes roll back into her head and she's unable to stay still.

I have to clamp down on my tongue not to cum. She can't be this turned on from throat fucking.

But she is.

To take my mind off the pleasure she's shooting straight to my veins, I lean back and find the valley of her sex.

I graze past the soft hairs, then to her clit. Her hips lift, seeking my touch. I circle the bud once, then slide my middle finger through her slit.

She's drenched!

Her juices coat my fingers, making my mouth water for a taste. I bring the finger to my mouth and groan around the delicious tang.

Her eyes open to meet mine. She pushes on my stomach and I withdraw from her mouth.

Eyes still on mine, she slides out from underneath me, then kneels and kisses me.

No. She licks my mouth open.

It's a mating of flavors. Her tangy mixed with my salty. It tastes so fucking good we both moan.

"I want to be inside you now." I don't give her a chance to respond.

I sweep her off her knees and lay her down, then I push her knees up to her chest and line my cock with her entrance.

Her mouth is still ravenous on mine. It's a good distraction because I doubt I can go slow.

I plunge straight to the hilt at once. Her scream gets lost in the kiss but her bucking lower body is sign enough that she likes this. She wants more, just as I do.

I go hard then, unable to stop myself. Her pussy is a maze I want to get lost in. Every thrust sends a new sensation slicing through my being. I never want to lose that feeling.

Her moans drag me out of my head. I open my eyes to take in her pinched features, her shivering body.

Her lips chant my name, but no sound comes out.

I know. I know.

It's too much. Too good.

I lean down and suck her lower lip, still keeping up with my thrusts.

Her legs open wider and I drop deeper. I go blind for a long minute. When I open up again, her eyes are glued to my face, as if she's searching for answers.

My heart beats faster as we stare at each other.

It feels more than just fucking now.

Every thrust seems to bind us tighter, and I'm not sure Maddie or I bargained for it.

I latch my lips onto hers and kiss her deeply. Her back arches and her fingers find their way into my hair.

I grind the base of my cock onto her clit until she's bucking into me, reaching for the feeling.

She's close.

Even though she's strangling me, practically wringing the cum from my cock, I wait until she's shaking and whimpering my name.

"I'm cumming, I'm cumming," she whispers again and again.

Just then, the repetitive clenching around my cock does me in. I cum, hard, flooding her channel. She takes it with bucking hips and moans, clamping down on me until the last drop is gone.

Then she falls back and I collapse on her, catching myself on my elbows at the last second.

I kiss her closed eyelids and she smiles.

My lips twitch and I fall to the side. She slides up to lay her head on my shoulder. I curve my right arm around her then with the left, I stroke her hair.

I'm not sure when it happens but soon, sleep claims us both.

***

I turn over to meet a soft body. My eyes split open and fall on Maddie.

The morning light trickles down her face and through her brown hair. She sighs and her lips part, a slight snore leaving her.

I trap the urge to laugh in my throat and smile instead. She claimed the sheets sometime during the night and she's all tangled up now.

I only keep from detangling her because I worry she would wake up and won't get enough sleep. But I can't resist pressing a quick kiss to her forehead.

Then I drag myself from her side to the bathroom. It takes a few minutes to clean up and when I get out, Maddie's up.

Her eyes clash with mine and she looks away. "Hi." She drags my shirt down to cover her body.

"Hi?"

She eyes me for a second. "Last night meant nothing."

I open my mouth to speak but she barrels on.

"It's just sex," she says firmly. "Nothing more."

"Fine." I nod, feeling my chest tighten.

She keeps her eyes on mine, waiting for more.

"I promise."

Satisfied, she looks around. "I'm guessing my off day is over. Can I get my clothes now?"

"They're in the laundry. Clean."

A smile plays on her lips. "Thanks."

The last thing I want is for her to walk out the door, but she does just that. And I'm left alone in the bedroom with the ruffled bed.

Chapter Eighteen

Maddie

I stop by Julia's desk to retrieve my files and laptop from the previous day.

"You're fashionably late." She grins. "What's up?"

I hide my blush by picking non-existent lint off my blouse. "Nothing. Can I get my laptop and my files?"

I don't need to look at Julia to know she's eyeing me.

The laptop and files hit the desk. "By the way, where's the boss?"

I snatch them up gratefully. "I don't know."

Then I spin away before Julia can ask me more questions.

I lock myself away in the conference room and catch up with yesterday's work—or try to. I can't get my mind off him.

I wasn't lying when I told Julia I don't know where he is. I left his home in my laundered clothes—when he got the time to clean them, I'm not sure. But I got back to the villa, cleaned up and changed into new clothes, and arrived at the office.

I expected to run into him but apparently, he isn't here yet.

Last night was wild. After the long day with him, I forgot everything I promised myself I wouldn't give into. And I did give in, hard.

I shut my eyes against the memory and bite my lower lip, resisting the urge to moan.

"A-are you okay?"

My eyes flash open to meet Lindsay's eyes. She works in the conference room sometimes too. Totally forgot that she's here.

I clear my throat. "Of course. Just trying to remember something."

She looks unconvinced.

I squeeze out a smile and face my laptop, but it doesn't take long for the words to blur out. And then I'm drawn into reminiscing about yesterday's events again.

The conference room door opens and shuts and I snap out of my daydreams again.

Tired, I sigh and hang my head.

This is what I tried to prevent. I can't get caught up in feelings. Just the thought of it causes bile to rise to my throat.

That's a recipe for disaster, especially since he doesn't feel the same. Taking me to the beach was simply a kind gesture, and afterward, fucking me to the height of ecstasy, that was... lust. That's all.

"Are you alright?" Lindsay asks again.

"What?" My eyes lift to her.

"You're not breathing right."

Jesus. "I think I'll just take a walk." I flip my laptop closed and step out into the hallway.

Faces blur as I pass by co-workers and head toward Julia's desk. She turns to me with a smile.

I smile back, hoping she has some tea about someone else to distract me from my conflicting emotions.

"Guess what?" She sits forward.

"Mm-hmm?" I lean over the counter, excited for something, anything.

"He's here."

"Who's here?"

"The boss." She smiles. "And he's acting as weird as you."

"Julia, you're imagining things." My heart is trembling, not because she's close to the truth, but because there's just a door separating Chance and me.

It'd be too easy to walk in now and get a sight of him. Maybe satisfy my prickling fingers with a touch across his broad chest. Would he let me?

"Maddie? Earth to Maddie." Julia snaps her fingers in my face.

I blink and settle my attention back on her.

"Are you even listening?" She frowns.

It's hard to catch Julia with a frown. I must be bad at hiding my thoughts. "I am." I smile, probably poorly because she comes around the desk and takes my hand.

She drags me off to the conference room I exited minutes earlier. "Lindsay, can you give us a moment of privacy, please?" The woman starts to speak but Julia smiles. "Thank you."

Lindsay rolls her eyes and struts out, complaining about not having a damn office.

Once she leaves, Julia turns the lock and faces me.

She crosses her arms and cocks a hip. "Spill."

"There's nothing to—"

"Really? You're going to keep pretending?" Her face falls. "We're friends, aren't we?"

"We are." I take her hands and squeeze gently. "But I can't make up shit that isn't happening."

It breaks my heart to lie to Julia, but I can't admit it to anyone. Not until I understand what's going on myself.

"So what was that about yesterday? Both you and Chance left for hours only to come back today with..." She scrunches up her face. "...secrets in your eyes."

"Secrets in our... is that Shakespeare?"

Julia laughs. "It's Juliaspeare."

"I think I like it."

"I know, right?" She bats her lashes with a smile.

I turn the lock and open the door. "You should do more of that."

"I will. Wait, are you trying to distract me?"

"Distract you?" I gasp, herding her out. "Certainly not." Once she's out, I wave. "See you later."

I shut the door and cave into myself. I only have to deal with all of this— the feelings, secrets, and pretenses for a week more. Soon, I'll leave Magic Island and be free of it.

That thought sends a sharp ache into my chest.

Do I really want to leave?

The door yawns open and I skip out of the way. Shit, Julia's back.

"I seriously wasn't trying to distract you." My eyes meet Lindsay's.

She has a *what the hell* look on her face.

"Um... I thought that was Julia." I turn away and head back to my laptop.

Finally, I manage to wrap up the report I'm writing.

Now, I have to get it to Chance.

Nerves churn in my belly as I head over to his office. Julia gives me a look as I pass by her desk. I ignore her.

Nothing is going on. It's simply a PA going to give her boss a report. That's all.

I close my hand around the door handle, take a deep breath and turn it.

Chance is not at his desk. He has his back to the office as he looks out the window.

Is he thinking about yesterday and regretting it? Or maybe he isn't thinking about me at all because I mean nothing.

That second thought should bring me relief. But it hurts, so bad. I want him to think of me, to want me. Not as an employee or a fake girlfriend but just me, Maddie Lowe.

"Are you going to keep standing at the door or are you coming in?" His stern voice tears through my thoughts.

I shake myself out of the fog of sadness trying to swallow me and shut the door. Then I head over to the desk, sliding the report onto it.

He doesn't look my way, gaze still fixed outside.

My pulse thrums. I don't care if his thoughts have anything to do with me. I just want him.

Without putting much thought into it, I cross the space between us and stand behind him. Then releasing a breath, I wrap my arms around his middle.

He receives my touch with a faint *oof*, probably because I'm squeezing him so hard. I ease up and he turns around.

His gaze is on mine, hand stroking my cheek tenderly. The feelings in my chest heighten.

I don't want to feel.

He cups my jaw and tilts my face upward, then lowers his lips to mine.

It starts slowly as he slides our lips together, with no tongue, just a gentle glide.

It lulls me to a comfort I didn't know I needed. I flatten my body against his and rope my arms around his neck, just feeling him.

Then his tongue prods my lips apart. I let him slide inside and roll around, find my tongue, and make them dance together.

Sensation pours through my body. A soft moan falls from my throat and I pause, alarmed that I'm taking it too far. If I sleep with him again, I'm sure I'll silence the voice of reason in my head permanently.

But Chance doesn't push for more. He keeps up the languid pace, his hand threading into my hair, rubbing tenderly, his kisses gentle and unending.

My heart thumps for him, for this. I rest a palm on his chest and feel him too. His heartbeat matches my rhythm.

Means nothing. It's just kissing.

It's just kissing. I tell myself this as Ralph drives me back to the villa that night.

There's a chill in the air I can't feel on my skin. All I feel is the memory of Chance's hands on my body, his skin pressed on mine.

I get into the apartment and lock the door behind me, then lean against it and sigh.

Just a few more days.

I make myself a chicken and veggies stir fry with baked potatoes for dinner. I'm eating at the table when I grab my phone and text Nat.

You up?

Her call comes through seconds later.

"Of course, I'm up. What's going on?"

I drop my spoon and sigh. "I fucked up."

"Oh, no. Maddie, are you pregnant?"

"No, what?" I gasp. "Why would I be?"

"Sorry, when you said that I just assumed—"

"Hell, no. Or am I?" I press my hand to my stomach. "Wait, no. I can't be. I've been taking my pills like I should."

"Are you sure?"

"Of course. Jeez."

Nat sighs. "Good, so what's up?"

"My blood pressure. Why did you mention a pregnancy?" I massage my chest. "I don't need more complications right now."

"I just meant— Wait, did you say more complications?"

"Yeah."

"Maddie," Nat says slowly. "What happened, doll?"

I tell her about the previous day and then the night.

"Yes, Maddie! Get it."

"No, no. Not get it."

"Oh-oh." Nat's excitement tanks. "Why not?"

"I have feelings for him, Nat. It's not fun or cute or cool. I feel things when I'm with him."

"Oh..." She's silent for a few seconds. "What kind of feelings are we talking about? Love feelings? Sex feelings? Friendly feelings?"

"The first," I whisper. "And the second too. The third is a given because he's so cool and fun and... The first worries me the most."

"Oh, Mads..."

"I'm so stupid. I should have known I can't do physical without wanting more."

"Hey, you're not stupid. You're just kind and sweet and you have a soft spot for everyone around you."

"I wish it's only a soft spot I have for Chance." I tuck my knees against my chin and rest my chin. "It feels like more."

It is more.

"What about him?"

I scoff, shaking my head. "What do you think? He's a man being a man. Of course, he'd take the sex and the kisses... But that's all it is to him."

"And you know that for sure?" Nat asks.

"I'm not going to put my heart on the line to find out. Just imagine the rejection." I exhale. "I just want this week to be over so I can get back home."

"You'll be welcomed with open arms. It's been too long since we saw each other."

That comforts me a bit. It's nice to know some things stay the same even when everything else is all up in the air.

"I'll be happy to, seriously. Magic Island has been nothing but spectacular, but I think my time's up. It's time for me to face my life once more." My voice tapers out on the last few words.

"Don't sound like that. It's not like Todd's here to bother you anymore."

I sputter a laugh. "Heard from him since the last time?"

"Nope."

"Well, at least that's some good news."

"Yeah."

A few beats pass as we're both quiet.

"Hey." Nat sounds perky like she's injecting forced cheer into her tone. "You'll keep yourself safe for me, right?"

"Yes, I will."

"I mean your heart, Maddie. I know Chance is a far cry from Todd, but I don't need you crying over any man again."

"I will. I promise."

I say so more to myself than to her. I only need to survive the next few days and then I'm up and away from here.

I'll finally be able to put Chance and these feelings behind me.

Hopefully.

Chapter Nineteen

Chance

The afternoon sun glares down on my neck and back as I make my way into Dad's home. The cool air-conditioning welcomes me and I sigh with relief.

"Dad?" He promised to be home at one p.m. today. Where is he now?

I poke my head into the kitchen and find Lucy by the fridge. Her mouth is stuffed with whatever she's eating. She grins and waves me in the general direction of Dad's study.

I give her a thumbs up and head that way.

His deep voice comes through the slightly open door. I knock before pushing it open.

He acknowledges my presence with a nod but continues speaking into the phone.

I take the moment to glance around the study. It's covered end to end with shelves that are brimming with books. Even his desk has no room, all covered in books about every subject known to man. A university would have a field day sorting through his books and enriching their libraries. Dad would never go for that though.

His books are his most prized possessions, next to his pictures of Mom. One sits on his desk now. It's a picture of them when they were both in their twenties. A few days before they got married. She has her arms wrapped around him, and a broad smile squinting her eyes. She was beautiful.

His hair is a deep brown here, unlike the gray streaks he sports now. His eyes are bright and I can almost hear the laughter they share.

I tear my gaze away to meet his eyes, watching me curiously. I didn't even notice when he stopped speaking.

His eyes leave mine and fall on the frame, then he picks it up. A sad smile tilts his lips as he rubs his fingers across the surface.

Emotion builds in my chest and nearly chokes me.

His eyes snap to mine and he smiles, then drops the picture face down.

Still, the damage is already done.

I leave his side to pace off the pain in my chest. It takes minutes, but finally, I feel alright, like I can face him again without breaking down.

I turn in his direction and his patient eyes irritate me. "I'm here about—" My voice is rough. Fuck. I clear my throat and try again. "Ramsey has decided on a campaign. I want your opinion. It's similar to the one he carried out while you were CEO but with minor adjustments he swears by. Just need your thoughts."

He slips on his glasses then picks up the document and flips through casually. "Didn't Maddie shut Ramsey down the other day?"

My heartbeat rams at the mention of her name but I manage to keep my tone neutral. "She did."

He chuckles. "I wish I was there for that." He closes the document and looks up. "How is she doing?"

"Just great." I step forward. "If you look at page 3, you'd see some ideas he has about publicity. I don't think that they will be very effective. But you may see the sense in it. I've been rejecting many of his ideas and I have to admit he has given this a lot of thought. I want to consider it. What do you think?"

Dad opens the page and squints. "What does Maddie think of it?"

"What does she—" I bite my tongue. "I didn't show her."

"But she worked in marketing before coming to the Island, yes?" He raises an eyebrow.

"Yes, but she is a PA right now."

"She's wasted as a PA, in my opinion."

"Dad, that's not the opinion I came here for." I stare at his serene expression, exasperated. "Can we talk about the campaign?"

He sighs. "Fine. Sit."

I keep standing.

"I won't speak until you sit."

I give in and drop into the chair opposite him. "So, what do you think?"

"I think you're too hard on yourself," Dad says. "You're trying so hard not to make mistakes when that's inevitable. As

CEO, you will make some mistakes. You will fund some projects that'll crash and burn."

"I know. All I'm trying to do is limit that."

"I know," he returns with the same cadence I used. "And I'm saying make the mistakes. Be a failure sometimes. Only with the ups and downs will you grow. You won't grow by running, okay?"

I fight the urge to facepalm. "Thanks, Dad," I drawl.

"So," he leans back, looking proud of himself. "When are you proposing?"

I'm still debating on my options with Ramsey's campaign that I don't understand his statement. "Proposing what?"

"To her." The *dummy* is silent, but I hear it in his tone.

I'm about to ask, 'Her, who?' when it dawns. I try to grab the document to hide my face in it. But he reaches across the table and snatches it before I can.

"Jesus, Dad!" I slap my hands on my thighs and lean back. "What do you want from me?"

"A date. A hint. Anything." He shrugs. "When is Maddie going to become an Easton?"

My heart clenches with that thought. "I don't know."

"You don't know?" He sits forward, looking more worried about that than the possibility of losing millions if a project falls through. "She's a lovely young woman. She likes you and you like her. What's holding you back?"

His question is bait, but I'm smart enough not to bite.

"That's not why I'm here."

He shakes his head, disappointment in his eyes. "You can tell me anything, you know that, right?"

"Of course."

"So, when—"

"Nope." I stand and take the document from him. "Not that."

"Fine. If you insist on not speaking about it, we won't."

"I do."

He sighs.

I'm almost out the door when his voice stops me.

"Have a closer look at pages 7 and 8. Ramsey can be too ambitious with the estimated outcome of his campaigns. If you keep the expectations small, you will be less disappointed. With that, you'll see how best to adjust the budget."

"Thanks, Dad."

He nods. "Take care. And if you see Lucy, tell her I'm still waiting on that lunch she promised me."

I picture her stuffing her face in front of the fridge. "Yeah, I'll do that."

I get back to the office forty-five minutes later. I lock myself in and get to work thoroughly reviewing the document. It's either that or obsess over Dad's words.

Does he hope I marry Maddie? He met her just once for fuck's sake. If he thinks that, then it's more than likely that Aunt Felicia and Lucy agree too.

I have no doubt Baxter would sign off on that, and Landon, he'll go along with it if he believes I'm happy.

I quickly shut down those thoughts. It doesn't matter what my family thinks. The thing between Maddie and I isn't real. She leaves in a few days and I have to move on.

Will my family move on, though?

I bury my face in my hands and let out a string of curses that'd draw a frown from Aunt Felicia. I fucked up.

If I never played into Baxter's game, I wouldn't need to do damage control at the end of this week.

I shake off the feeling that I'll be making the worst decision of my life by letting her go.

They'll be fine.

Will I?

I ignore that thought and resume working.

I don't notice that the light is fading until I glance back at a text and can't make out the words.

Behind me, the sun has fallen beyond the horizon and left traces of pink and purple in the clouds.

I turn away and switch on the lights, then resume pouring over the documents before me, making adjustments and recommendations.

A knock brings my head up. There's a kink in my neck I ignore.

A second passes and then Maddie walks in. She's still here? I snatch my wrist up and check the time.

"You're still here?"

She shrugs. "So are you."

"That doesn't answer my question."

Her lips tick up. "Fine. I'm still here. Can you see me? Or am I a ghost?"

I walked into that one. I allow her a moment to smile to her satisfaction. "You shouldn't be here so late."

"Neither should you."

Her gaze roams over my face, then a frown pinches her brows. "You look exhausted."

She comes closer, blessing me with a view of her pretty features and curvy frame.

She doesn't stop opposite me. Her heels click on the floor as she rounds the desk.

I swivel to face her, leaning back to get a good look. Despite being focused on working all day, my brain shuts down and my body hums to life at her nearness.

But she's not looking at me like that. Her frown deepens as she leans in close to my face.

I pull in a breath of her and my limbs weaken. Then she does the last thing I expect, she pushes her fingers into my hair and massages my scalp.

My eyelids lose strength and stay closed, and my whole being hones in on the slow, gentle touch.

"Maddie," I murmur. "What are you doing?"

"Does it feel good?" she whispers.

"Yes."

How didn't I know I needed this? I lean forward into her touch and rest my head on her stomach, holding onto her waist as she lulls me with her fingers.

She finds a spot just below my ear that makes me fucking purr.

Her laugh vibrates in her belly. "You need to rest, Chance. You work yourself too hard."

My muscles tense. Rest isn't for me. "Someone has to do the work."

"That's why you have employees. You can't keep doing this day after day."

My rebuttal dies on my tongue as she rubs down my neck to my shoulders.

"Hmm?"

"Yes," I blurt.

"You agree?" There's a note of surprise in her tone.

"Yes."

Anything she asks right now, it's a yes.

"So... you'll stop working for the night?" She circles a spot at the base of my neck.

It takes a few breaths to say yes, just so I don't sound like I'm moaning.

"And you'll let me take you home?"

"Yes."

"Huh. Car keys?"

I pull out the drawer.

She starts to take her hand off my hair.

I grab it and replace it.

"Oh, okay. I just need one hand to pick up the keys." They clink as she does. "And then I need my hand back so we can leave the office and I'll drive you home?"

"Okay."

I let her hand go. I miss it instantly, but I swallow the urge to complain.

She grabs me by the arms as I stand, her face turned up to take me in. "You good?"

I press a kiss on her cheek. "I am."

Her smile warms me. She threads her fingers in mine, and with her other hand, she shuts down my laptop and picks up my jacket.

I normally have my laptop to continue working at home but Maddie doesn't give it a second glance as we walk out of the office and lock the door.

My car is the only one left in the parking lot. She opens the door and waves me in, a smug smile on her face.

I roll my eyes and get in, then she gets in next to me and heads out.

It's unusual for someone else to lead while I sit back, but right now, it's welcomed. I lean back and shut my eyes, only jerking awake when her hand prods me.

"We're home," she says.

I get out of the car and Maddie comes around to wrap an arm around me. Not that I need her help to stand upright or walk into the house. But it's nice to feel her soft touch.

"You're taking this very seriously," I comment.

"Of course." She turns up her chin. "I'm a very serious PA."

Laughter rumbles through my chest and she smiles.

"Do you want something to eat?" She turns on the lights in the living room.

"No. Bed, then you'll do that thing with your hands?"

She quirks her lip. "Yes, sir."

Chapter Twenty

M addie

Chance's body is made of hard muscles borne of discipline and a strict lifestyle.

Hell, I don't know why he's letting me hold him. Despite the exhaustion lining his eyes, he looks as though he'd manage to get in bed alright without my help.

I press a hand to his arm to stop him and open the room door. I meet his eyes and they're watching me with a curious expression.

Yeah, yeah. He once had me on my back and pulled whimpers from my lips in this very room mere nights ago. But that's not why we're here.

I pull him to sit on the edge of the bed. He follows my lead and sits quietly with his hands on his thighs and his head down.

My heart squeezes. He looks like a year's worth of stress is pressing down on his shoulders.

I lean in and kiss his face. His hands come up to my hips and start a slow caress, and as I go lower, his breath comes out heavier. Mine too.

No, Maddie.

I draw myself away and offer him a small smile. We're not doing that. Instead, I kneel and reach for his buttons.

He lets me take them off, then shrugs off the shirt. Off comes his inner shirt next. Then he takes off his shoes, rises to his feet, and takes off his slacks and socks.

He's in only briefs.

My eyes are saucers in my head.

It's hard to push aside the part of myself that just wants to push him on his back and writhe in his lap.

I tear my eyes from that tall glass of temptation and meet his gaze.

He's so tired.

"Come on." I pat his chest and ease him back down onto the bed. "Lie back."

He does as I ask—head on the pillow, hands on both sides of him, and his eyes on the ceiling.

I sit next to his prone figure and rub my hands gently up his chest. It's smooth but firm and breaks out in gooseflesh beneath my touch.

I glance at his face to make sure this is alright. He's giving me a soft look. So soft my heart melts with it.

I look back down to where my hands are tracing up the strong column of his neck to his jaw. He groans a sound in his throat and then closes his eyes.

My thumbs go up and down the lines of his jaw, while the rest of my fingers rub the underside of his ears. For the grand finish, I work my fingers into his hair.

He sighs and turns into my touch. My lips curve with a small smile, and I run my fingers through his hair, tracing different patterns to give him comfort.

Slowly, his breathing turns heavier, and his eyelids stop fluttering. I press a kiss on his cheek and he doesn't react.

Even though there's nowhere I'd rather be right now, I need to work tomorrow. I withdraw and pinch the edges of the covers at the bottom of the bed and drag them up.

He turns over, facing the ceiling once again. I'm careful not to stir him too much so his sleep is not disturbed.

I'm tucking the sheets around his chest when my fingers graze his skin. He makes a sound in his throat and grabs my hand. It's a firm hold. I frown at the spot.

But then with my left hand, I work my fingers into his hair, then press a kiss to his forehead.

His hold relaxes but he doesn't let go. "Don't leave."

My brows furrow. He's asleep, right?

He places my hand flat on his chest and I feel the thump of his heartbeat.

"Don't leave," he says again.

A blush heats my cheeks. I stay that way with my hand on his chest. A smile plays on my lips. I planned to call Ralph and have him take me back to the villa, but right now, what's the harm in staying? Chance asked me to.

"Mom."

My brows go up. *What?*

"Mom," he says again. "Don't leave me."

I withdraw my hand and fold it in my lap, watching his features. That isn't about me spending the night. It's about his mom.

But why? I remember the awkwardness around the subject of his mom that night. There must be something there. I need to find out and lay this curiosity to rest. Once and for all.

Julia is jolly at her desk the next day. She has earphones plugged in and she's moving from side to side.

I pull one of the earphones and she turns around with an affronted look. It quickly changes to a smile as she sees it's me.

"Hey, you. What's up?"

"Do you know where I can find Baxter?" I look around the office. He's like a mirage—everywhere and nowhere. I only run into him randomly and have never heard anyone mention an office attached to his name.

"Oh, he'll be with the clients in the game room."

"What?" My brows go up. "There's a game room."

"Mm-hmm." She nods, then shuts her eyes and dances in her seat. Probably lost in her song again.

"I'll leave you to that." I start to walk away.

She gives me a thumbs up and yells the direction of the game room.

I don't believe it until I find the door labeled 'Game Room.'

The hell? We didn't have a game room where I worked back home.

What's the protocol?

I glance from side to side, then decide to knock before pushing my way in.

It's like I've stepped into a different dimension. Music plays from a surround sound system, and staff sit casually on sofas having glasses of wine and chatting.

True to its name, there's a dartboard in a corner, a ping pong table, a miniature golf course, hoverboards, and a foosball table that two people are going hard at right now.

My shock fades as I recall why I'm here. I find Baxter in an area that looks like a mini-living room from its setup. Two sets of chairs facing each other with a glass coffee table in between.

I cross the room toward him. His eyes lift and brighten as they fall on me. He says something to the people he's talking to and rises to meet me.

"Maddie, I didn't expect you in the fun corner of the building."

"I didn't know it existed!" I look around. "How is this allowed?" I spy the head of sales throwing darts. "How..."

He catches my gaze and shrugs. "For morale and shit like that."

My eyes narrow. "It was your idea, wasn't it?"

He grins proudly. "You know me too well, Maddie. Now, what can I do for you?"

I glance at the conversing men he was with moments ago. "Julia said you were with clients, but..."

"Whatever reason you're here bothered you so much you didn't mind interrupting."

"Yes. Do you have the time?"

"I think I can spare a few minutes." He excuses himself and speaks to the men, then returns to my side. "I'll find us a quiet spot."

He leads the way out of the game room to a room covered end to end with shelves that carry documents. There's no one here but us.

He stops and turns, nodding. "What's up?"

"It's about Chance," I admit.

"I knew this day would come."

I frown at his smug smile. "What?"

"No, no. Ignore all of this." He gestures at his face. "Just lay your heart bare."

"Lay my heart— What do you think is about to happen?"

He laughs. "It's not about what I think. It's about what's meant to be."

"I have no idea what you're insinuating."

He tries and fails to rein in his smile. "Sorry, I won't rush you. Take your time. Tell me everything."

"Okaaay." I give our surroundings a cursory scan. It's only us. Sighing, I spill. "Last night, Chance said something when he was about to sleep. 'Don't leave me, Mom.' And he has been awkward around the subject of his mom—your mom. I know she passed but I don't understand his reaction and I think it's only you that can tell me why that is."

Baxter's smile falls until there's nothing left but severe lines and a tight frown.

"Baxter?"

He looks away from me. "I'm sorry, Maddie. Whatever you noticed, take it up with Chance yourself. It's not my place to say."

He starts to move around me. What the hell? I catch his arm, forcing him to stop. "Baxter, what is it? Did something bad happen? Why can't you tell me?"

He sighs, his broad shoulders sinking. "I'm sorry." He extracts his hand easily from my hold.

My heart crumbles. Whatever this is, it eats deep into Chance, and apparently, Baxter too. If I let him go, I'll never know and never understand Chance more.

You're leaving, Maddie. What does it matter?

It matters. So fucking much. It hurts to see Chance pained and broken, and that's how he looked when we spoke of his mom. I need to get to the bottom of this.

I go around Baxter and block the exit to prevent him from leaving. "Baxter, please. I need to know."

"Then maybe ask him?"

"He won't tell me."

Baxter's gaze drops because he knows I'm right. Hell, I can almost imagine Chance shutting down if I broach the subject.

"Please," I press. "I care about him and I want him to be alright. If there's anything I can do, then I'd like to know."

Baxter meets my eyes and I know he has caved. He reaches behind me and turns the lock on the door, then leads the way deeper into the storage room. He sits on the desk and points to the free chair.

I take it dutifully and keep my eyes on him. He looks at me for a long minute before sighing.

"I know this will come back to bite me in the butt, but here it is." His eyes carry a faraway look and I hold my breath so I don't interrupt. "My mom, our mom, was diabetic. There were times she was alright, and at other times it hit her hard. During the last episode that claimed her life, Dad, Landon and I weren't on the Island. But Chance was. Dad kinda told him to take care of Mom. It was just a statement." He shakes his head. "Chance was a twenty-one-year-old back for the holidays and having fun with his girlfriend. He didn't know."

"Didn't know what?"

Baxter shakes his head as if willing the thoughts away. But his eyes dim with the memory. "According to him, he was out having a good time with his girlfriend. Just being silly young people. When they returned to his car, there were numerous calls from Mom's number. He rushed to the house to check on her, but the paramedics were already there. She was already gone."

"Oh, no." I press my hands to my lips, my heart breaking.

"He always blamed himself. If only he wasn't out having fun, he could have been there for Mom. If only he was more responsible. A host of if-onlys. For months, he wallowed, blamed himself, and hated himself. When he came out of it, he was different."

"Different how?"

"He was far more focused than any young person his age had a right to be. Since then, he has worked himself to the bone, as if trying to pay for what he says is his fault. He denies himself everything remotely pleasurable." His gaze fixes on me. "Even a woman to love."

I push aside the feeling that crops up in my chest at those words, certain he doesn't mean me. Just some woman, any woman.

That's why Chance always seems out of reach.

"Till today, he still punishes himself. That's it, Maddie. That's my brother's story."

The lock jiggles and someone knocks.

"That's our cue." Baxter heads out and opens the door.

I follow behind him in a daze, unable to shake off the words he said.

We walk past a woman who gives us a curious look, but I couldn't care less. The only person I care about has been in torment for all these years. And now my heart hurts too.

Chapter Twenty-One

Chance

Maddie has been missing all morning. Unusual. But I don't have time to look for her.

I have an impromptu meeting with the CFO and Ramsey, going over the campaign budget. We've managed to cut it down but the CFO still raises eyebrows at the numbers Ramsey quoted. He's adamant we can't spare that much.

Now, Ramsey is forced to go back to the drawing board. And he's not very happy about that.

I tap his shoulder on the way out of the CFO's office. It's nothing personal, just business. He dips his head in a nod, his shoulders down. I'm watching him walk away when my eyes lift.

There she is.

Maddie stands in the hallway speaking to a staff member who I don't give more than a passing glance. All my attention is focused on her.

She's in a cream-colored dress with black detailing. It looks soft from a distance and tempts me to hold her in my arms, breathe the fragrance from the slender slope of her neck and run my fingers through her bouncy brown hair.

I imagined I'd wake up with regrets today. Being vulnerable has never been my strong suit. I keep everyone at arm's length. That way, I feel most in control.

Last night, I gave in to the need to be looked after for once. And damn, it felt good. I woke up more rested than I've been in... forever.

And it's because of Maddie.

She's still engrossed in her conversation, her face tilted up. An occasional smile plays across her animated features. I feel an answering smile tick my lips. She draws it from me even without trying.

I'm glued to the spot, watching her, unable to tear my eyes away.

"Mr. Easton?" a voice draws my attention.

I glance sideways, then back up.

Maddie's gaze snags on mine. She looks away quickly and rushes off.

A frown pulls my lips down. Where is she off to?

Pulling my gaze away from her, I focus on the person who spoke to me in the first place.

Once that's over, I attend to other duties.

It's late afternoon again when I catch a break and go in search of her.

This is the first day since she started here that I have hardly seen her. And I'm not alright.

I was seconds from quitting the meeting early. It took all my willpower to push aside the feeling and sit through it.

Glad to be done now, I march the hallways, seeking her out. I do a mental calculation and cross into the hallway leading to the conference rooms. Julia once mentioned she'd set Maddie up there. I've never had to find her, until now.

I slip by a room and spy through the mottled glass a shoulder-length hair bowed over a laptop.

I trap the relieved sigh in my chest and push the door open. Maddie's not alone. Two other staff members glance up from their work as she does. They fall over themselves with greetings and I only nod in their direction, my eyes on her.

She wouldn't look at me.

"Maddie?"

Her gaze lifts to mine. "Yes, sir. Is there something I can do for you?"

The fuck? Why does she sound so professional?

I can't remember a time when she has spoken to me this way. Is it because we have company?

"Excuse us."

The other two exit the room and then we are alone.

"You can drop the act now." I stick my hands in my pockets.

Maddie frowns. "The act?"

"You know." I huff a breath. "Acting like you're the most professional PA in the world."

It's meant to be a joke, but a line forms between her brows, deepening her frown. "I am professional."

"I didn't mean it like—" Now, I'm apologizing. I bite my tongue and backtrack. "Did you have a good day?"

"I did," she says and rises.

A stupid part of me thinks she's coming over but then she picks up her purse and starts to fit her phone and stationery into it.

She's leaving? Crap, um... "Have dinner with me."

Her eyes connect with mine. Whatever she sees makes her lips turn down. "I'm sorry, I can't."

My eyebrows lift. I thought for sure she'd like to go out with me. After last night, seeing the way she cared, I hoped—

Fuck it. I shouldn't have. Still, her mood can't be my fault, right? I couldn't have fucked up between last night and today. I wrack my brain. Nothing I've done jumps out as wrong.

Purse all packed up, she slides out of the space between her chair and the table, and then she's headed my way. For the door, no doubt.

I stand to the side, watching her. She throws her gaze sideways, somehow more interested in the glass walls than me.

My heart fists in my chest. I can't let her leave like this.

She's passing by me when I reach out a hand. She sucks in a breath and scoots away from my touch as though my hand is on fire.

Our eyes meet and I have no doubt my look betrays my shock. She shakes her head in a non-answer, looking deeply hurt, then she leaves.

What the actual fuck?

My heartbeat is all wrong as I eventually pull myself together and follow her out. I spy the tail of her dress as she slips into the elevator. The doors pull close with a finality I hate.

Tomorrow, I'll get down to the bottom of this, whatever it is.

Like the previous day, I don't see Maddie in the morning. She's meant to report to me. I don't want to pull the boss card, but she leaves me no choice.

Plus, my poor sleep last night brought on by wondering what was wrong with her has made me cranky.

I forgo using the intercom to ask her to come into my office. A walk will help clear my head before I speak to her in my current state and say something I shouldn't.

I stop by Julia's desk. "Where's Maddie?"

Julia's eyes shift suspiciously. "She's occupied. I can send her to you once she's available."

"She's my assistant," I bite out. "What is she occupied with that doesn't have to do with the work I've assigned her?"

Her gaze drops to the polished desk surface. "She's downstairs."

Why is she being weird?

"What is she doing downstairs?" Julia purses her lips. I crane my neck, considering. "Who's she with?"

Her face shoots up. "I didn't say a name, did I?"

"Well, I'm asking for one."

She swallows. "She's with her ex," she admits quietly. "He showed up and asked to see her."

My stomach clenches. Is this the cheating ex? The one who hurt her so bad she'd get physical with a stranger to forget him?

I should go back to my office, focus on anything but Maddie. But I'm a glutton for punishment. I head for the elevator instead.

It reaches the first floor and I step out, my eyes seeking her out. She's not hard to spot. Her brown hair stands out, rich and full. A silky blouse sits above a form-fitting skirt that hugs her hips and reaches down to her shapely calves.

She's so beautiful my throat closes. I take measured breaths to center my head.

I came here for a purpose. To see for myself that she's with him. The ex who broke her.

I tear my eyes from her lovely frame and look beyond her.

A man stands before her. He's brown-haired with blond highlights in the short waves, wide shoulders trapped in a jacket and boots on his feet.

As he speaks to her, he raises a hand to play with the tips of her hair. Maddie catches his hand and doesn't let go. He twists his wrist and curves his fingers around hers. They're holding hands now.

Maddie gestures with her free hand. Something she says makes him laugh and he pulls closer to her. Their angles shift and I'm getting their profile views now.

They look just right together.

Both are from the city, both have lives to get back to. Maybe what happened was just a minor hitch in their relationship. He's most likely here to win her back and they'd go back to being in love and... I'd lose her forever.

She was never mine. What am I thinking?

But she was once his. His eyes are warm and searching. I know that look. It's done by a man who wants a woman. A man who wouldn't back down until he's had her.

And Maddie…

I pull my gaze away. I know what I'd see. She'd be into it for sure.

I back away and spin to the elevator. My finger burns as I long-press the button. I want the quiet of my office to get my head in the right place. To forget whatever stories I built about us in my head.

Everything we've had is a tryst. Just fun. Nothing more.

I can't get to my office fast enough. Once in, I shrug off my jacket and drape it over the back of my chair, then I head over to the window and look out over the city.

I pull in measured breaths. My mistake was forgetting who I've always been. Giving into feelings, pretending I'm someone who can be cared for—foolishness. I'm done with that.

In mere days now, Maddie can leave and everything would go back to the way it's always been.

I exhale, glad to have my head back in the right place.

The door yawns open and heels click on the floor.

The resolve I've built cracks with every sound.

I shut my eyes, pushing down the hurt rising in my chest.

"You called for me?"

Her voice shakes me to my core. It undoes everything, releasing the hurt. It fists my heart and seeps into every part of my being.

How can she sound so calm when she knows what she has done?

Fuck, I'm unraveling.

"Chance?"

Her voice is sweet, soft torture.

I swallow, struggling to get myself under control. She made no promises to me. I can't expect her not to do as she pleases. And if it pleases her to get cozy with her ex, then so be it.

I turn around. I'm smacked by her confused expression.

She has no right to look so fucking innocent.

"Quick. What's on the calendar for today?"

"Oh, um..." Her eyes turn up in thought.

"Really? You don't know?"

"No, I just—"

"Got a little distracted? Forgot to do your job?"

Her brows furrow. "Why are you speaking to me this way? I didn't remember to bring my laptop along and I moved around the hours a bit just this morning. That's why I don't have it in my head."

"Or could it be another reason, don't you think?" I frown. "Maybe you saw your ex and other things are now occupying your mind."

Her mouth falls open. "H-how do you know that?" She shakes her head. "Doesn't matter. I'm here now, and I'm doing my job."

"Oh, what you did just now? That's doing your job?"

"What's your problem?" Maddie steps forward, irritation pinching her features. "Is this about forgetting your calendar? I can go right now, memorize and regurgitate it to impress you. Will that make you happy?"

"I don't care about that shit, Maddie!" I press my fingers to my forehead and pace to get my thoughts together. Doesn't work, so I spit it out. "Is he the reason you refused to have dinner with me last night?"

"What?" Her face scrunches up. "What are you talking about?"

"Your fucking ex! You want him back, don't you? That's why you're pushing me away."

Once the words leave my mouth, I know I've said the wrong thing.

Maddie's face falls.

I open my mouth to speak but there's nothing to follow that up with. She's staring at me, her lips trembling. I can't look away now. She looks crushed. I feel the same.

It's out there and there's no going back now.

Chapter Twenty-Two

Maddie
Did he just say that?

I can't believe the day I'm having. First, I turn up at work and I'm tasked with reorganizing Chance's already-packed calendar. It's a hassle, calling to reschedule meetings.

I'm done when Julia calls my attention. Someone's asking for me downstairs. When she says Todd, my stomach bottoms out.

I tell her to tell the downstairs receptionist that I'm not available. There's a back and forth and Todd threatens to make a scene if I don't show up.

With my heart in my throat, I head down. I'm not nervous to meet him. He means nothing now.

It's just a memory of the life I've ignored for three weeks catching up to me. Seeing him brings back those memories and they don't leave me feeling very good.

Only to come up and meet this accusation.

I bite my lower lip to stop the trembling and look away from Chance. How can he think that I want to get back with Todd?

"Look at me." His voice is warm and husky and commanding.

I hate the way it pours over me and makes me feel fuzzy on the inside. He has no right to make me feel conflicted.

On one hand, I'm mad at him for his senseless accusation, on the other hand, I need him. Trying to stay away from him is self-torture. Yesterday was a lesson in how I'm taken with him.

I refuse to think about what would happen when I leave.

Right here and now, I need him and I'm mad at the same time. He has no right to accuse me of getting back with Todd so I channel my anger and push away the desire to lose myself in his arms.

"I can't believe you'd say that." I meet his eyes. "You know what happened between me and him. How can you say I want him back?" *You should know how I feel for you.* The words are stuck in my throat but I'm not going to say them. He'd probably toss them back in my face.

I'm sure he's going to say something biting back. But he drops his head. "I just thought... when I saw you two together. I can tell he's still into you."

"And what if he is?" I draw nearer to him. Which means I have to tilt my head back to meet his gaze. I don't care. I just need to look into the blue depths of his eyes and see if he's fucking with me right now.

"What if?" I challenge. "I'm not dumb, Chance. I know what he did and an apology doesn't change that. He's apologizing for his conscience or whatever, but it doesn't change that I'm over him." *And now, I'm into you.*

Shut the fuck up, Maddie.

Chance looks back up, his chest moving as he exhales. "So, if he's not the reason you've been ignoring me, then why?"

Uh-oh.

"Um…"

His eyes shutter. "Are you lying to me?" The hurt in his gaze shatters my heart. "If you want him, you can say it. You're leaving anyway and I won't blame you if you want something familiar to get back to."

I'm shaking my head, but he continues speaking. Keeps saying those words that crush me over and over, like he believes it.

"I get the attraction." He shrugs. "I won't judge. You can do as you will. Don't just lie about it."

"I'm not lying!" I'm a pitch from yelling, but I can't help it. I close the distance between us. Up close, every breath I take is coconut and coffee. This is all I want to breathe, not Todd's cologne. *This*. "That's not why I stayed away. He has never meant anything to me." *Not since I met you*. I gulp. "Please, you have to believe me."

"Then why?" His tone is rough, his eyes searching mine.

My shoulders fall. He won't believe me unless I give him a reason for my actions yesterday.

I press my eyes shut knowing I mustn't. But if I don't, then I risk breaking his trust. Taking a deep breath, I blink open. "I… I…"

"Maddie," he grates. "Let's just—"

"No!" I press my hands to his chest. His heartbeat pumps beneath my touch. "I stayed away because I felt hurt, okay? I learned about what happened to your mom, your hand in it, and I couldn't bear to look at you. Because I… I felt so bad that you'd feel that way and I was scared that if I spent time with you I'll bring it up and…"

His frown gives way to a look of pure horror.

He's mad at me.

I yank my hand away and step back. "I'm so sorry. I shouldn't have." Moisture sips from my eyes and hits my cheeks and my voice trembles. "It wasn't my place. I'm sorry, Chance. Please…"

A sob breaks from my throat and the weight of everything crashes down on me.

I bow my head and my shoulders tremble. He hates me now for sure and then fucking Todd pushing everything to be out in the open. Why didn't I ignore the idiot? Or send him off once I met him?

I'm still going over my should-haves when firm hands touch my shoulders and travel up and down my arms. It's a comforting gesture that reduces my sobs to hiccups.

I tilt my head and meet Chance's gaze. There's warmth in his eyes and something else I can't place. I sniff and his shoulders fall with an exhale.

He thumbs away the traces of tears on my cheeks, his eyes following his touch.

I wish he'd speak, tell me it's alright, but he does none of that.

His fingers drop to my chin, then he swipes his thumb over my lower lip. He does it again, caressing slowly, then applying pressure.

My mouth pops open and a sigh releases.

A sound vibrates in his chest and he closes the gap between us. His body is flush against mine, eyes roaming my face.

It's a chore on the back of my neck to keep my gaze up on him, but I can't look away.

He circles a hand around my back allowing me to relax, just a bit. Then his head dips.

My heart flutters in my chest, my lips tingling with anticipation.

He drifts down slowly, as if debating with his actions, but finally, his lips touch mine.

I'm not sure what he was going for, but once he touches me, I know need like I've never felt before.

I take his lips, feeling the soft, gentle press. It's both assuring and arousing, making me hot for him.

I run my hands over his shoulders and up into his hair. His hands splay on my back, pressing me closer into him.

It's not enough.

I lick his lips, moaning as his tongue touches mine. More. His tongue darts past my lips and finds my tongue.

It's a wild, savage dance how he kisses me. Our breaths are harsh, our bodies pressing together like we would sear off our clothes if we could.

"I need you, Chance," I gasp into his mouth.

He answers by trailing his hands down my body and fisting my skirt. He drags it up, then pushes his hands underneath.

My skin burns where his hands grab and knead. It's almost painful how his fingers dig into my ass. But I want more.

I tear my lips from his and lick his earlobe, then his neck.

He hisses, craning, giving me room. I bite.

"Fucking hell," he growls.

I reach for his collar to pull off the shirt but he catches my hands in a tight grip. He pushes my hands apart, then spins me around to face the desk.

"No," I start to turn. "I want—"

"Stay." He presses into me from behind.

I inhale sharply. His rock-hard cock notches between my ass cheeks. My body trembles as I realize only my lace underwear and the fly of his pants separate us.

I forget I want to feast on his skin and instead, roll my hips against his hard length.

He groans roughly, then his hand lands on my shoulder and pushes me down.

My cheek hits the cool desk, my waist curved, ass in the air for him. I'm unable to move. But I want to.

I try to brace my hands and rise, but he growls and takes my hands, trapping them at my lower back. His left hand holds both of my wrists in a tight, constraining grip.

"Chance," I whine. "I want to participate."

I can't believe it's something I have to ask for, but he doesn't answer.

The sound of a descending zipper fills the air and my body shudders with anticipation.

I want to see him, touch him, and know he's not mad at me. But he doesn't let go despite my struggles.

I'm about to speak again when the heat of his bare cock grazes my ass. Wetness floods my pussy, my walls contracting and releasing rhythmically, eager for him to fit into me.

He takes his time, rubbing his cock up and down the stretch of my slit through my panties. His breath hisses out of him and I have no doubt he's getting an eyeful of my soaked panties, while all I have in my view is the door.

I wiggle around, circling my hips so he gets the idea. I want him inside.

Finally, he pulls aside my panties. Before I can take a bracing breath, he plunges deep inside.

"Fuck!" He presses into my back, curving around me, and sinking deeper.

I exhale, trying to get used to being filled. Turning my head to the side, I'm met with the view of us in the window. It's faint, but it's there.

My pussy spasms at the picture we make.

Chance's pants are stuck around his knees as if he couldn't be bothered to take them off in his haste to fuck. His pelvis is flush against mine, his cock buried deep inside me.

My eyes are wide and unfocused with lust, my lips slightly parted as I pant. I mouth a curse as he pulls back. His cock comes away slick with my juices, then he crams himself right back in.

A cry leaves my throat and my eyes fall shut. It's one thing merely feeling what he's doing to me. It's another seeing his face veined with concentration, our bodies separating and coming back together with loud smacks.

I bow my head and receive his thrusts, biting my lips so I make no sound. A soft kiss flits across my neck and I can't help my whimper.

How can he fuck me so hard and kiss me so soft? It's a combination that's breaking my body and my heart.

He licks me in that spot, then nibbles playfully. Tears seep from my eyes.

"Oh, Maddie." He groans and kisses my cheek. He gentles his thrusts, hitting it just right.

My pleasure heightens, giving me something to focus on other than the heaviness in my chest.

I throw my hips back to meet his thrusts, rolling around a couple of times.

Chance lets my hands go and lifts from my back. He grabs my waist and helps me back into him.

Moans fall from my lips as our combined efforts make it better. My legs can't stay still anymore.

I turn over and see the glass image again.

Chance is looking down at where we meet. His mouth hangs open, his eyes half-mast.

He increases the pace, slows down, and then goes fast again. He groans as my body quivers.

Flattening my palms on the desk, I plant my feet and impale myself on his cock as hard as I can.

"Jesus, you want it." Chance presses his head to my neck, then works a hand between my legs. He finds my clit and fingers it. Slowly.

"Faster, please."

He does as I ask. It doesn't take long.

A scream tears from my throat and my body trembles violently. I grab the edges of the desk to hold steady as the orgasm whips through me.

Almost immediately, the heat of Chance's seed spills inside me. He grunts, fucking my clenching pussy a few times before sinking deep as he can go and holding his cock there. As if he wants to imprint my womb with his cum, mark me as his.

The thought whips my senses into place. I'm not his.

His body sags against mine, his breathing heavy. I rise, dislodging him.

He falls a step back and I step away. I pull my panties up and tug my skirt down.

"Maddie, are you okay?"

I give him a passing glance. I've experienced a rollercoaster of emotions because of him. And he asks me that?

"What do you think?" I eyeball him, then march out of the office.

Chapter Twenty-Three

Chance

My hands twitch on the steering wheel. I look out over the newly mown lawn to the front door. A window by the door is lit up, as expected. It's only eight p.m. She's still awake.

I half hoped to find all the lights off. Anything to make me turn around and go home, give myself the excuse that she isn't available.

But that lit-up window mocks me.

I need to talk to her.

Yet, my body won't move. Oh, I know what to say—the truth. Would she take it though? Would it mean anything to her?

I take a peek in the side mirror. No one's coming behind me, or coming up ahead. I'm the only one out tonight sitting in the shadows like a stalker, watching her villa.

Pushing out a breath, I let the steering wheel go. I grab the fresh flowers I bought up on my way over.

Dirt crunches beneath my feet as I make my way up the walkway, onto her porch and knock.

She might as well slam the door in my face as soon as she sees it's me. I know I'll deserve that. Heck, I'll take that over talking.

The door opens.

My throat closes.

Maddie stands before me in an oversized t-shirt. Her hair is packed up and away from her face and a sheen of wetness covers her lower lip, like she was in the middle of dinner when I knocked.

"I got you flowers." I extend the bouquet.

Her gaze drops to it. She doesn't move for a long time. Then finally, she takes it. "Thanks."

She's still not looking at me.

My heart fists. I knew to expect that she wouldn't accept me with open arms. It still hurts to know it for certain.

I glance at our surroundings, then back to her. "May I come in?"

Her gaze whips up to me. "Why?"

"Just to talk." I swallow. "I want to tell you everything."

Maddie bites her lip, contemplation in her gaze. A beat passes and then she steps to the side, still holding the door open.

It should be a relief that she gave me an audience at all, but my stomach twists.

I would have to admit things I've kept to myself all these years, but she deserves that much.

Remnants of her dinner sit on a plate on the coffee table. Once the door closes, Maddie skirts around me to pick up the plate.

"Make yourself at home." She waves at the living room before leaving.

I take a seat on a too-fluffy cushion and wait.

She returns with neither flower nor plate and drops into the chair opposite me. Her legs fold beneath her and she crosses her arms. She looks serene, but only a complete idiot would miss the hurt heavy in her eyes and the defiant tilt of her chin.

"What's everything you think I should know?" she says.

I fix my gaze on my palms, rubbing them together. They'd rather be planted on her skin, pulling her into my lap and smelling the soft, warm fragrance of her skin. But right now, a table separates us, as well as my secrets have.

"My mom—" My voice cracks. I clear my throat and try again. "My mom was the sweetest soul. She had a way of making everyone and everything better just by being present. She loved Dad, supported him, and she was his life."

The skin of my face tightens as moisture builds behind my eyes. I quickly shake my head.

"Her only weakness was her illness. Diabetes runs in her family. We all knew that growing up. There were times when she'd need days to a week to get herself back after falling ill. Dad made sure she had all the medical care she needed, and we boys were prepped on what to do if any crisis arised. Heck, even Landon knew at just eight."

Memories float through my head, tugging at me. I focus on only what Maddie needs to know.

"He loved her very much and protected her."

I exhale the air trapped in my lungs, still looking down at my hands. I'm not sure what I'll see if I meet Maddie's eyes. This could all mean nonsense to her.

When it's eating me alive.

"We did love her too," my voice breaks.

I was the oldest. I got to experience her the most out of all my brothers. I got to feel her love and care and scolding, and all the other great things that made her special.

And I took that away from them, especially Landon.

"Until I failed everyone." The words suck the breath out of me. I entwine my fingers together to keep my emotions under control.

"I came home for the holidays and Dad promptly assigned me tasks to keep me busy at the company. It was a nice challenge, but I also wanted a break. So I took it on that Saturday morning. The previous day, Dad had taken Baxter and Landon for a weekend-long trip off the island for a school competition. They were to return on Sunday. Saturday was the only break I had from Dad's pestering. So I tossed my phone and went to the beach. Something didn't sit right but I chucked it up to guilt that I wasn't working. I should have known."

I bury my face in my hands, willing the thoughts to recede. But they are a part of me. I've replayed them a thousand times over the past years.

How I failed Mom. How I failed Dad. How I failed everyone.

I'm a fucking failure.

"I saw the calls when we got back to the car. I rushed home as quickly as I could but—" *Deep breath.* "The ambulance was already there. She was laid out on a stretcher. They were zipping up her body."

Agony knots deep in my heart and pain claws up my throat. I swallow my tears with rapid breaths.

"It was all my fault. If only I'd done what I was meant to do. If only I stayed where I was supposed to, then she'd still be here."

"You don't know that," a whisper cuts into my monologue.

My eyes lift to meet Maddie's.

Her face is wet and her lashes carry beads of liquid.

She is crying... for me?

My heart collapses into my stomach. I don't want her tears or sympathy. I want her to tell me I was an idiot, that I was wrong and foolish and failed everyone. And I deserve nothing good.

"Yet, it happened. Here we are."

Her lips turn down. "You can't keep blaming yourself, Chance."

"Then who's to blame? I should have been there for her."

"No." Her brows wrinkle, eyes softening. "The stupid genes that allowed her to have diabetes are to blame. The lack of a permanent cure is to blame. Don't take that burden on yourself."

I huff a sound. The burden is the only thing that defines me now. It's my motivation. I'd never fail anyone else, because I'll do what I commit to do.

"I've poured myself into my work, Maddie. That's all I can do now. It makes me—"

"Worthy?" she snaps back. "You think that's what your family needs from you? You think that's what absolves you?"

"I'm not looking to be absolved. I can never be. I only want to pay back."

"You won't bring her back, no matter what you do."

Her words hit me where it hurts the most. "No."

"Yes, that's the truth, Chance." She sits up and leans forward. "I'm sorry. It breaks my heart what you went through, but it feels worse knowing this is how you have dealt with her death."

"I've made it work so far."

"No, living half a life isn't making it work. Working yourself to the bone isn't making it work. Choosing not to be happy?" Her throat bobs and she looks away. "That isn't making it work."

I say nothing. She's just like the rest of my family. For the first few years after Mom's passing, they tried to tell me how to live. Tell me to slow down, go easy on myself.

But they don't realize when you go easy, that's when people you love die.

No, that's no way to live. The way I do it, that's the way.

"Look," her voice coaxes my gaze up. "I can't tell you how to live, but from the little I know, I don't think your mom would want you to keep punishing yourself, Chance."

I bow my head. What do I do then? Go on as if nothing happened?

"Please?" Her voice shakes. "You don't have to live in the past. You can acknowledge that you weren't available when she called. But you can also acknowledge that you need to live outside that guilt and pain."

I wish I could, but I don't know how.

"You need to get help," she says.

I lift my head.

"Talk to someone? I don't know. Something. Anything." She exhales, moving her head from side to side. "Like this, you're not good for yourself, and I doubt you'd be good for anyone else."

My chest tightens. "Maddie..." Is she rejecting me? Just because I feel guilty that my mom died doesn't mean I can't feel other things. And I do, I fucking feel a lot for her.

"You need to heal, Chance." She squeezes her eyes shut but a tear escapes and lines her cheek.

I want to wipe it off, kiss her and make it better.

"For someone else," she says.

What? "No." I gulp. "I can do better. I will."

"I don't think trauma this great can be fixed in a couple of days." She bites her lip.

She's referring to her departure.

I don't argue against that. Right now, I'm not sure what I feel.

When I say nothing in return, she wipes her eyes and rises to her feet. "I need to go to bed for tomorrow."

I'm out the door when I take a full breath. It's cold and flower-scented. Head down, I take the stoned path to my car.

I glance out once I'm behind the wheel. The light in the window goes off.

The finality of it fills me with dread. I thought I'd lose her when she left, not now. Not because I'm not worthy.

I hit the gas and move. I can hardly make out the road before me, lost in my head as I am.

I thought holding my guilt over Mom's death and working as a recompense would make me accepted. Just to get a rejection because of that.

A mirthless laugh cracks from my throat. But then I sober quickly.

My family told me. Dad stood by me when she was lowered into the ground. He placed his hand on my shoulder, squeezed. Aunt Felicia held me and promised she was a shoulder to cry on. My brothers and my cousin stayed close to me, even as kids, they cared. They saw I was broken and tried to help.

I expected to be disowned. Not doubly loved and supported.

I broke down three nights after, crying before Dad. He hugged me and told me he didn't blame me.

"These things happen," he said as if it was nothing.

As if I didn't rip the family apart.

Guilt dug its hold into my heart and never left.

I drive to a stop outside my home. Getting out of the car, I look up. The stars are out tonight, dotting the sky like a million diamonds. Mom used to say that.

I sigh and lean against the door, staring up. What would she want?

I can imagine Mom scolding, asking why I'm so grumpy.

Why are you punishing yourself, son?

I deserve it.

Do you?

My jaw trembles. I clench my teeth.

I'm tired. The weariness sits deep in my bones. I want a break from all of it—the pain, the shame, the guilt.

"I want something different."

I suck in a breath, watching the sky. Mom would want it too. She'd forgive me. I know this.

I want to forgive myself too.

I have to.

Can't go on this way.

I'll forgive myself. For the sake of my family and for Maddie's sake.

Chapter Twenty-Four

Maddie

I tuck myself under the sheets and try to sleep. It's useless.

First, it's too early. Can't remember the last time I slept at nine p.m., if ever. Secondly, I can't keep Chance out of my head.

It took all my willpower to keep from holding him tonight, telling him it'll all be fine, that I was here for him. I wrapped my arms around myself instead and kept them there.

Though I could feel his hurt, it was not my place to heal. It's his. He has to come to terms with what happened, admit to himself that taking the blame for something that happened fifteen years ago does him no good.

And me? I have to go home.

What am I even doing here? Pining after a man whose guilt overshadows everything else and has taken over his life.

I doubt he can feel anything else apart from the pain in his heart.

Why does the fact make him all the more appealing? I just want to help, but I can't. I shouldn't.

If his family couldn't get through to him, who am I?

I turn over and look out the window. The sky is bright tonight, covered with twinkling stars. There's never a night this clear in the city. Always all fogged up with fumes.

A tear chokes in my throat. I'm going back.

In three days, the three-week arrangement with Chance will be over. For the past week, I've tried to block it out and ignore the inevitable. But that's not happening now.

Todd's presence served to make matters worse. Or more real, depending on the angle you look at it from.

I sigh and kick off the sheets, suddenly feeling warm. Even though it's tempting, I don't open the window to let in the breeze dancing through the trees.

That night plays over in my head. Someone was trying to get in and I'm not going to make it easy for them. I turn up the AC instead.

Then it's too cold and I tuck myself back underneath the sheets.

I shut my eyes and it's... Chance.

"Fuck." I flop onto my back and stare up at the ceiling.

I can't be this hung up on him, can I? But I am.

I list all the reasons I shouldn't be, ticking off my fingers.

He's not ready to be in a relationship.

He hasn't even asked me out.

I'm leaving.

I can't forget all of these. If I do, then I may contemplate something stupid. Build castles in my head that'd come crashing down when faced with the harsh reality.

I need to survive Chance.

Tomorrow is the last day I'll be working with him. I'll put my head down and earn the final cents he'd pay me. That's why I stayed, isn't it?

I roll over to the cooler side of the bed and force my eyes shut. I push away thoughts of Chance, and then a particular nagging thought flits into my brain. I sit up and drop my curtain. Can't be too careful.

For the past week since the incident at the door, I haven't had to look over my shoulder. Chance promised to keep me safe, and I am.

He has cared for me, made sure I'm provided for, gone above and beyond...

Since I'm his employee, I remind myself, then force myself into a dreamless sleep.

"Hey, Maddie!" Julia waves me over.

I just arrived at work and I'm heading to the conference room. Today, I've decided to limit my meetings with Chance as much as I can. To make the break on Monday much easier.

I head her way. "Make it quick." My eyes stray to Chance's door, then the elevator. I don't want a surprise.

"Okay, ma'am." Julia gives me a look. "So, guess what?"

"Wow, erm…" I eye her. "You ran out of foundation and had to borrow your sister's?"

She gasps, her eyes wide. "Is it obvious?" She snatches a tiny mirror out of her purse and strains to see her face and neck. "Oh, no."

"Julia, stop!" I laugh, despite myself. "You look pretty. I was only teasing."

She drops the mirror and gives me the stink eye. "You're such a rock-licker."

"What's that?"

"Oh, it's a snail that's always lying on rocks and crawling over them. That's what the kids call it. Rock-licker."

"And you know these kids, how?" I frown.

"That's what I was trying to tell you before you brought up the damned foundation!"

I press my hand to my mouth to stifle my laughter. "Sorry."

Julia flips her hair. "Anyway, I have a date this weekend."

"Oh, my goodness, that's amazing!"

"Yes!" She clapped her hands, her eyes bright. "He's a dad. Two kids. Absolutely adorable."

"I'm so happy for you." I lean across the desk and hug her.

"Yeah. I have to replace you since you'll be leaving me."

"Aw, really?" I withdraw to take her face in. Her eyes are sad. "I'm sorry."

"Nah." She waves a hand. "I'll just go back to how things were before you."

"No." I tweak her cheek which earns me a frown. She's very particular about her makeup. "You'll have the new PA to bond with I'm sure. No one can resist your sunshine personality."

"New PA?" Julia scoffs. "Like that would ever happen."

What? My brows draw together. "Why, I thought Chance would have a replacement lined up by now."

"What are you talking about a replacement?" She lifts her mirror, takes in her features, and smacks her lips. Satisfied, she fits the mirror back into her purse. "There's no replacement."

"Um, what?"

"What?"

Ugh. I sigh, placing my laptop on the desk to relieve my arms. "Someone has to do my job when I'm gone, don't they?"

Julia looks at me like I'm crazy. "No, not really." She shrugs. "I'll handle part of it and Chance will cover the rest."

"Um, no." I squint. "How can you say that? There was a PA before me. Surely, you're going to want to go back to that."

She shakes her head. "Where are you getting this from? I and Chance have been managing just fine. There was no PA."

"No." I shake my head. "He told me himself that there was a PA and he wants me to cover for them since they left. He needed me to work for three weeks then he'd get a permanent replacement."

"Babe, no. Why did you think I fell in love with you the second you reported in? You relieved me from work I've been doing since forever. There's been no one else."

"But he told me."

For the first time, her brows furrow. "Maybe you heard wrong?"

"I know what I heard. He said—" Oh, no. My insides twist.

If Julia is saying one thing and Chance said another that means someone's lying. Julia has no reason to lie to me.

But Chance had every reason to... to keep me here.

I meet Julia's gaze. Her face has lost color like she realizes it too.

"He..." I swallow. "He lied to me."

"I'm sure he had a good reason." Julia stands and places a hand on my arm.

I pull away, pacing. "He lied to me."

"He has always needed an assistant." Julia rounds the table and grabs my arms to stop my movement. "Maybe that's what he meant," her voice trails off. Even she doesn't believe that tale.

"Julia, where is he?"

Whatever she sees on my face makes her shake her head quickly. "What if we just calm down first?"

"Where is he, Julia?"

She bites her lip.

I turn away and go to his door. It's locked. "If he's not in yet, I'm going to find him."

I start across the floors toward the elevator and she calls out, "Conference room."

I turn to her.

"He had an emergency meeting so he came in super early." Her shoulders fall. "He's in the conference room."

I head in that direction.

"Maddie?" Julia's voice halts me. "Please, be careful."

I'm done being careful. He lied to me. I was vulnerable with him, admitted my deepest desires and fears, and he just lied so flimsily. Like it's nothing.

Hell, I may have taken the job regardless of whether he had someone for the job before or not.

I needed the money, but I also wanted to be close to him.

But he'd gone with deception, played on my emotions, and made me believe I was fulfilling a valuable role.

Fuck me.

I've been a joke this entire time. No wonder everyone looks at me like I'm a stranger here. I was never needed, just shoehorned in.

Tears catch in my throat as I reach the conference room door. I swallow it down. There's no time to feel pity for myself, just anger at being played.

That's all I can allow now.

I close my hands around the door handle and turn. All eyes turn my way as I step in. I look straight ahead, keeping my gaze on him.

His face is lined with exhaustion but his gaze picks up as I come in.

I push away the warm feeling, seeing him up after the night he no doubt had. I can't have sympathy for him. He deceived me.

"You lied to me."

"Maddie, what are you doing?"

"You lied to me." I enunciate every word. "I believed you. I was a fucking fool."

"Maddie." His tone is held back thunder. "You are interrupting an important meeting."

"I don't care."

"Leave." No one moves a muscle. "Now!" he barks.

Chairs scratch the floor as the staff rises and scurries out.

Once they're all gone, Chance levels me with a steely gaze. "This had better be good."

"You lied about the fucking PA position!"

He looks clueless so I explain. He can't pretend not to know what he did.

"You told me you had a PA that left when that's a blatant lie. There was no one, and there'll be no one after me."

His eyes shutter, but he doesn't look away.

"Can't deny it now, can you?" I spit. "Oh, goodness."

I run my fingers through my hair and pace. How was I such a fool?

I should've linked all the little clues, but I was too busy getting lost in Chance's eyes to actually think.

His handwriting was in all the notes I received. There is no actual office or designation for the PA. He manages just fine most times and I have to force him to abdicate my duties to me.

"Why did you lie?" I face him. His jaw flexes, but he doesn't speak. "Was it to keep me here? To be your fake girlfriend? To decorate your office? To be the joke of the entire building?" I gulp back tears. "Well, you got what you wanted, but I'm done."

He flinches.

"I'm done with all of this!" I gesture around us. "I quit. You can keep your fake PA job and your fake everything!" I yell, then storm out.

A tear leaks out of my eye. I dart a hand and wipe it off but another quickly replaces it. I hurry past Julia, ignoring her when she calls out.

I need to get away from here. *Away from him.*

Chapter Twenty-Five

Maddie

I strip my clothes off the hangers in the closet and toss them in the open suitcase on the bed. Half of them spill over the edge and the rest lie haphazardly in the suitcase.

Ignoring the mess, I go for another set. My hands shake as I toss them in the suitcase.

Slips of clothes still hang in the closet, but I don't care. I'll find where to fit them later. I just need to know I've gotten my bags packed and ready to go.

A bitter tear catches in my throat. I swallow it down and force my shaking hands to keep working.

I stuff the clothes in the suitcase and punch down, then I throw the lid over it and drag it so the edges of the zipper line up.

I pull the zip, but halfway through, it gets stuck. I lean over the lid, eyeing the spot.

It's caught on a dress.

Shit.

I tug on it but it stays stuck.

"No. Fuck." I try to pull out the offending fabric, but then it rips.

The sound is loud in the silence. I stare at the torn dress and tears start to roll down my face.

"No!" a sob rips from my throat.

Why did he have to lie?

I fall back on my haunches, burying my face in my hands. Warm tears slip between my fingers and my shoulders tremble.

With every expression of hurt, my heart breaks all the more. Why am I so fucking hurt?

It's just a little white lie, right? Whether he said so or not, I'd have stayed. Just the salary would have convinced me.

Yet, here I am—the utter fool. I wasn't even needed. Just there to be mocked. Everyone surely knew Chance didn't need me. I was just there on his fucking whim.

A fresh sob coughs up my throat. I drop onto my ass and place my head on my knees. It hurts so badly to be used that way.

But why does the thought of leaving hurt worse?

I'll be without the island, the colors, the cool air on a warm day, the sweet fragrance all around me, and *him*.

How can I feel so hurt, but miss him so damn much?

I don't want to be mad at him. I'd like to spend the last moments of my time on Magic Island in his arms, not here, mad and broken.

I shake my head and wipe my eyes. I can't think like this.

He deceived me and made me fall for him. Thoughts of him shouldn't control my emotions.

I pull myself up and head for the back door. It's late evening and the sun hangs low in the sky. Though nearly dark, the air is still warm and it prickles along my skin.

I breathe in deeply before heading off. I'm not sure where I'm going, but I need to walk, get out of my head.

I'm drawn toward the hotel resort. It's a beacon in a sea of low buildings.

A few people stream by me as I follow the trail that leads to the hotel. I finally break into the garden.

There's a live band playing cool jazz music and bright-eyed folks dance to the rhythm. It's similar to the party Nat and I attended when we showed up at Magic Island for the first time.

My heart clenches. That was the first day I met Chance. He helped me in the elevator, and I cradled his jacket like it was a warm hug. I never imagined I'd have anything with the man.

And now... I see him everywhere I go.

I shut my eyes and whoosh out a breath, trying to get lost in the music. It doesn't work. All I can think about is him, and leaving.

I don't want to go.

I try to shake off the thought by walking some more. I shouldn't want to stay, there's nothing for me here. Even the job I have and would have begged to retain is a sham.

And the man who could grant me that is a liar.

If someone told me the person who was my knight in shining armor would become this deceptive, I wouldn't have believed them. He seemed good through and through.

You never know people, right?

I wipe the tear that dances down my cheek and stare at the night sky. It's filled with stars like the night that Chance brought me to see the gardens.

My gaze drops to the path that leads away from the main courtyard. It tempts me, lures me.

I remind myself I'm not seeking a connection to Chance, just a reminder of happier, more innocent times. Before I fell for a deceiver.

I break away from the party and take the lit-up path. It's ethereal walking down it.

Every step reminds me of those moments with Chance beside me. And now there's no one, just the sounds of the night to keep me company.

I zero in on the chirping crickets and the gentle sway of the tree branches, letting it soothe me.

The sounds of the party fade, as does the sunshine. Darkness swallows everything by the time I make it to the inner garden, but the fountain bubbles with light shining from within.

Warmth threads through my heart as a flicker of hope threads through me. If I can still find little things beautiful, then I'm not completely broken. Just bent.

A sad smile ticks up my lip. Tears come down, but they don't break my heart. I wipe both cheeks, glad there's no one here to see it.

It's just me, and the memories.

I'd miss this hidden garden, the island, and my friends. Julia and Baxter's faces flash through my head.

A laugh bubbles up my throat. Julia's always pumped for everything and Baxter always found a way to push Chance's buttons.

And Chance always played right into it.

Despite how he reacts, I doubt he minds Baxter too much.

I could have sworn I caught him smiling once when Baxter was acting up. And then the day we played tennis at his house. He had been a different person then, much like the person that took me to the beach.

He was free and laughed easily. And happy.

Knowing now what I do about his mom, it makes sense how he held back. How he resisted being anything but serious.

My heart squeezes for him. The only thing I can hope for is that this period has impacted him positively. And it'd remain so.

Even if I won't be here to see how it turns out.

I force a smile, despite the sad lump that grows in my throat. Soon enough, I'll be up and away from here, and everything that has happened would be history.

Leaves crunch behind me.

My heart leaps into my throat. Someone's here. Maybe it's him. Just the way I was drawn here, maybe he is too.

I turn around. My eyes catch on the blond highlights in brown hair and my heart plummets. "T-Todd?"

He steps forward. "I'm here, babe."

I frown at the smug look in his eyes. "What are you doing here?"

My gaze snaps left and right. It's only us. But how's that possible? I asked him to leave when he showed up at the office.

I wasn't interested and I wanted nothing from him. He agreed to leave, but here he is. How?

"Came to see you, babe." His eyes squint, head tilted. "Isn't that obvious?"

"Last you told me was that you're leaving Magic Island."

"Well, I decided not to. Not without you anyway."

"Excuse me?"

Todd draws nearer. I'm too shocked to move and the moment he stops before me, his heavy cologne claws up my throat. I only keep from gagging because his fingers run down my cheek.

"Are you... crying?"

I slap his hand away. "It's none of your business."

He chuckles. "You don't know how much of my business you are, Maddie. But you'll learn soon." His eyes roam my face. "What happened? Did your boyfriend break your heart?"

"How do you know about him? And he's not my boyfriend." My brows pull together. "Doesn't matter." I shake my head. "It means nothing to you. Just leave!"

"No." He catches the tail of my hair between his fingers and rubs it. "Not without you."

A sick feeling fills my stomach. That's the second time he's saying that.

"I'm not leaving," I bite back. I won't give him the satisfaction of knowing Chance and I fell out.

"Then I'll have to force you, won't I?" His eyes flash in the dark.

Fear molds around my heart. Todd was the boyfriend I had just because things aligned that way. I'd grown to love him, but that faded as time passed—as I realized he was nothing but a user. I did all the work, funding his life, and he was content to half-ass everything.

Then he cheated on me and I couldn't hold us together anymore.

In all that time, he'd never terrified me like he was doing right now.

"I'm not going anywhere with you," my voice cracks.

"You don't understand, do you?" he snaps, pressing close to my face so his breath fans my skin. "Your former bosses contacted me and asked me to bring you back. You've gone rogue. They've tried to reach you through emails, but you're not answering."

"They fired me," I protest.

"Well, good news for you. They want you back."

"I'm not going back to work for them. You can tell them that." I fold my arms across my chest to hide the shivers pouring through me.

"You cheeky little thing," he sneers. "You are coming with me. You think a simple no would make me leave?" He chuckles wickedly. "You've always been stupid."

"Why are you doing this, Todd?"

"Money, babe." He rubs a finger down my cheek.

I can't help my reaction. I lean away from his touch and his eyes darken.

"I need the money. You're not there to complete your part of the rent, so..." He curves his fingers into a fist. "I'm going to get it somehow. Quite interesting that the person who took my comfort from me would be giving it back, isn't it?"

"You're selling me out? You bastard! You were the one who cheated. You fucking broke us up!"

He rolls his eyes. "So fucking dramatic. Just because you found out that one time!"

"There were more," I whisper, touching a hand to my chest.

"What do you think?" He glances at his watch. "I'm done playing catch up. Time to go."

He wraps a hand around my arm. "Let's go."

"No." I tug but fail to dislodge him. "I'm not going."

His fingers dig into my arm, painfully. "Fucking move."

"Todd!" I yell. "You're hurting me."

"And I'll do worse if you don't cooperate."

"No." I dig my heels into the ground.

He yanks.

My shoulder hurts in its socket but there's no way I'm willingly going with him.

He raises a brow, his eyes darkening with the realization. "Fine, we'll do it the hard way then."

He whistles.

What is he...

Dark figures pour out of the press of trees around us.

Fear clamps down tight on my heart. It's them. I'm not sure where to go so I pull closer to Todd, still looking around at the men closing in.

Todd smirks.

"You are with them." My mouth drops open.

This entire time... my stalkers have been from my former job and my ex.

I have to escape. But the men surround me now. If I go forward, it's Todd and behind me, it's them.

I'm trapped.

Chapter Twenty-Six

Chance

I whoosh out a breath as I tear through the night to Maddie's villa. I know the last thing she wants is to see me, but I have to try. I can't let her leave without making up somehow.

I turn down the lane that leads to her home and ease off on the gas. The car slows to a crawl and stops in front of the wooden home. The light is on inside.

An exhale falls from my lips. The deja vu is heavy. Except for the absence of flowers, it's like the last time.

This time, I don't dawdle. There's no time to waste. Best to get over with the rejection quickly.

I climb out and march up the walkway, then I stop at the door. I knock once.

There's no answer, so I knock again. She doesn't answer.

Has she seen me through a window and decided she doesn't want to talk?

I push away the hurt that fists around my heart. "Maddie, we have to talk."

It's completely silent. No shuffling, no rustling.

Is she even in?

I turn the lock. It doesn't give. Proud that she's still careful about her safety, I round the house.

The back is possibly locked too, but I try it anyway. And it opens.

My brows draw down. She should be more careful than this.

Just so I don't spook her by creeping, I stop at the door and call out her name. The villa isn't tiny, but it's cozy enough that sound travels easily. She should have heard me by now.

Worried now, I make my way into her home. "Maddie?"

There's no answer. She's not here.

Where would she be then?

I glance around and my eyes fall on her phone. If she left her phone that means she's close by.

I step back out into the night and look up. The hotel resort stands bright at night.

She's in the garden. Our spot.

Certainty crests in my chest.

I hurry back to the car. Is she there because she misses me? Wants to connect to what we shared?

A lump forms in my throat. That means she feels something. She may be angry, but she doesn't hate me. At the very least.

I can work with that.

I tear into the hotel parking lot and hop out of the car. Guests mill around leisurely. I hurry past them earning some scathing looks, but they roll off my back.

I'm here for her, no one else matters.

My heart thuds in my chest as I hurry to the inner garden. With every step, I know I'm right. She's here.

It just seems natural to come back here after everything we've been through in the past weeks.

I race to a stop at the entrance. My chest heaves, my eyes taking everything in. It takes a few moments for my eyes to adjust to the dim light, but once they do, my shoulders fall.

No one's here.

The fountain bubbles, the crickets chirp, and the breeze sings through the trees. Everything is as it was that first night aside from Maddie.

I guess I don't know her as well as I thought.

I drop into a bench and bury my face in my hands. Look at me, acting like a lovesick fool. There's no *our spot*. It's a stupid garden and I'm—

I squint. Right next to the fountain, the grass is disturbed. I'm off the bench in a second and crouched close to the spot.

The lawn looks distressed as if feet dragged on it.

I blink against the thoughts forming in my head, but they persist.

"Maddie," I breathe her name.

She was here and something must have happened.

I stand and look around. There are no clues apart from a torn-up lawn. I'm being foolish playing detective, looking around for clues.

But she's never been truly safe here. The security team watched her, but what if for some reason they missed her and someone got to her first?

Anger surges in my chest. I hurry out of the enclosure and look left and right on the main path.

Which way would they have gone? Then my gaze snags on a blue piece of cloth hanging onto a thorny shrub. It's in the opposite direction from where I came.

I hurry to it and squat, picking up the cloth. It's jagged as if ripped off from a larger piece. I rub it between my fingers. Soft and flimsy like the ones Maddie favors.

They have her.

I resist the urge to break down. She needs me.

Pulling in deep breaths, I take my phone out and dial the head of the security team. "Where is she?"

"She's at home. We've been watching and—"

"No, idiot," I grate. "She's gone."

"No, can't be. We've been monitoring. You're the last to go to the front door—"

"The back door! Were you watching the goddamn back door?"

He doesn't answer.

"Come to the hotel. Someone has taken her. I'm going to follow the trail I've found. Stay close to your phone. I'll update you on what I find."

I end the call and start on the path. It's steep and plunges into darkness. I hurry along, not caring.

Maddie is in danger. That's all that rings in my head. Over and over. I failed her once before, I can't fail her again.

The path ends and I fall into an open field. I look around. I've lost her—

Hushed sounds reach me. Across the field, hidden in the night, there's a car and four people hurrying over to it.

Even in the dark, I can tell it's her.

I quickly call the head of security and update him on my findings, then I take off running. I draw nearer and my heart shatters.

They have Maddie by her upper arms and they're pushing her into the car. Her mouth is gagged and all she can do is scream muffled sounds.

The back passenger door opens and they push her toward it. She wedges her feet on the sides of the door, resisting.

"Fuck, Maddie! Just let them put you in the damn car," a voice says. "There's no use struggling. No one is out here to help you. You'll only hurt yourself."

Somehow, her gag dislodges and she yells. "Fuck you, Todd! And fuck this! I'm not going with you."

Pride swells my chest at her defiance. But also anger as I hear who's behind all of this. Her ex. The man she told off. He wants her against her will? What kind of sick bastard does that?

I don't delay for a second longer. I'm on them in two long steps.

Before they can make sense of the fifth person among them, I grab one of the men who has his hands on Maddie. I hold him back by his collar and yank him backward.

He doesn't expect the force since he's so focused on manhandling Maddie. His feet give way and he drops a few feet away, dropping her.

The other man curses and holds onto her. "Who the fuck are you?"

My answer is a punch to his nose. It's absorbed by the cloth mask covering his face, but he still staggers from the force. Maddie takes advantage of this, raises her leg, and comes down on his foot.

He yells and lets her go.

She runs into me. "Chance, you're here." Her eyes search my face as if she can't believe it.

I spare a second to hold her close, assuring myself she's alive and well. If she wasn't... I push away those thoughts. Now's not the time. "Run."

She looks back at the men struggling up and her ex watching us with narrowed eyes, his chest heaving. "I can't leave you. They have a gun."

"Go, now!" I push her behind me and don't look back, eyes on the men. "Leave, Maddie."

I only breathe again when I hear her footsteps recede.

The three men snarl at me.

"You're making a mistake, buddy," the ex, Todd, says.

"No," my voice is chilly like the wind now whistling around us. "It's you who has made a mistake."

Even though they're three against me, his face shutters with fear. What a wimp. He was never worthy of Maddie.

The first masked man comes for me. He's the one I dragged off Maddie. He's still strong and fast and I'm only able to evade two out of his three punches.

The one that gets me in my stomach makes me double over. Todd's jeers pull me back up. I retaliate with a punch of my own.

The force of it vibrates in my arm as my fist collides with the man's jaw. He staggers backward. I don't let him recover as I kick his midsection. He sprawls on the ground and the next masked man takes his place. This one flashes a savage grin and moves in before I'm prepared. He clips me in the jaw and my head flips back.

Maddie's cry fills the night. I glance up to see Todd looking her way. Wanting to go get her? Not when I'm here.

Though aches and pains are working through my system, I push them back. I catch a few hits but eventually immobilize the man. He's flat on the ground. The other man stirs, but they are not my business. Not right now.

I race across the field and catch Todd just as he's nearly on Maddie. I tighten my arm around his neck in a chokehold. He strains and scratches at my arm.

"Maddie..." he gasps.

"Don't speak to her." I tighten my hold. "You will never have her."

He kicks back, but I evade his flimsy attempts.

Maddie watches us. Then her eyes widen as she looks behind me. "Chance, watch out!"

A force slams into me almost immediately. My hand loosens and I'm forced to let go. I turn around to see one of the masked men with a gun pointed at my head.

Behind him, Todd is bent over retching. "Kill him. Kill the bastard and get the girl."

"We have our orders. No murders." He looks behind me to Maddie. "Come with us and no one has to die."

"She's not coming with you," I say.

The gun clicks ominously.

"Chance." Maddie's voice trembles behind me. "Maybe I can just—"

The sounds of cars tearing toward us end the conversation. We all turn as headlights spotlight us.

Help is here.

Before the men can make sense of what's happening, I run for Maddie, carrying her out of the way. The cars don't stop heading for the masked men.

The gun starts to go off at the car, but it's useless. One man realizes this and starts to run, but the car slams into him and his buddy and they fall to the ground.

It's satisfying, but there's one left.

I turn just in time to see Todd heading for us, an ugly look on his face and a war cry spilling from his lips.

The fucking fool.

I push Maddie to the side and press my fingers to my palm. Just when Todd is close enough, I raise my hand and punch him in the nose. He tumbles to the grass unceremoniously.

I stare at him as the security team hops out of the car. Some rush to the men while the leader comes to me.

I raise a hand to halt his apologies. There's no use now. What's done is done. "Get all you need to know out of them and clean up this mess."

Maddie comes to stand next to me. "Todd says my former company contracted him to bring me back."

"Really?" I eye her. "Then it's over for them." To the man, I say, "Get to it now."

Once he leaves, I allow myself to face Maddie. Her eyes look strained underneath the moonlight.

"Oh, Maddie." I tug her into my arms and she lays her head on my chest. "It's over."

Her hands wrap around my midsection. "I was so scared."

"Shhh." I rub up and down her back, breathing in the sweet fragrance of her hair, feeling her warmth. "You're alright. Everyone who had a hand in this will get their due recompense, I promise."

Finally, Maddie stops shaking and takes a step back. "Thank you for this." Her eyes meet mine.

I know there's a *but* coming and it crushes me.

"But I'm leaving."

"No."

"You can't keep me here," she says.

Of course, I can't. If I force her, I'd be no different from the men that harassed her tonight. So I go with the only card I have left to play.

"We had a deal and it ends on Monday. It's not over yet. You have to keep your word."

Her eyes stray into the dark, her eyelids blinking rapidly. She can't deny it. I've got her—but only until Monday.

The unpleasantness tightens my chest. I don't want that to eclipse the short time we have left. "Let me take you to your villa."

Her gaze meets mine, soft and vulnerable. "Okay."

I throw one last glance over my shoulder to see the team putting the men in the car. Soon enough, we'd know all we need to and then it's payback time.

Maddie is quiet on the ride back. When we stop in front of her villa, she gets out. She walks stiffly up the walkway. I climb out too.

She rounds the house and enters through the backdoor, nearly shutting the door in my face.

I catch the door with one arm and follow her anyway.

She heads to her room. "Don't you have somewhere to be?"

I don't like the way her voice sounds like she's barely holding in tears. "I want to make sure you're fine."

"I am," she snaps.

Her tone doesn't deter me. She walks into her room and I catch the door, closing in behind me. Then I come to a stop.

"I promise I'm—" Her eyes meet my face and follow to where my gaze is fixed.

Her clothes are piled up in her half-closed suitcase. She's already packed?

My eyes connect with hers.

She shakes her head quickly. "It's not what you're thinking. I…"

"You were going to leave without telling me?" Does she hate me that much?

Her lips tremble.

Even if I'm never going to keep her, I want this moment. I close the space between us and cup her face, looking into her eyes. Her gaze drops to my mouth.

I give into the feeling and dip to take her lips. She receives my kiss with a soft moan, her hands going into my hair. She's kissing me like it's the last time and my heart breaks into a million pieces. But I push away that hurt and focus on what she's giving.

I kiss her lips slowly, savoring her taste. Wanting to feel more of her, I trace her arm, but then she winces. Frowning, I withdraw and my eyes fall on the reddened spot.

Anger squeezes my chest. Must have been where they held her.

"I'm sorry I wasn't there soon enough."

"You came. That's all that matters," she whispers, then her brows furrow. "How did you know where to find me?"

"I came to see you and you weren't here. So I guessed you must have been in the garden by the fountain."

I expect her to smile but she frowns. "You have to go." She pushes against my shoulder.

She doesn't want to settle what's wrong between us. That much is obvious. I don't bring it up.

"We're still on for dinner tomorrow night?" I ask.

She firms her lips and nods. "And we have to break up."

I meet her eyes. She means every word.

It was over anyway.

"Fine, we will."

"You won't back out this time."

I swallow. "I won't."

I have no idea why she manages to look more hurt. It's what she wants, isn't it?

"Good." She presses out a smile. "Goodnight."

And just like that, I'm dismissed.

Chapter Twenty-Seven

Maddie

I decline Chance's offer to pick me up on Sunday for dinner at his Dad's. I wouldn't survive the twenty-minute ride without breaking down. Already, I dread what we were going to do tonight.

I wipe my moist hands on my dress. It's a teal gown that hugs my skin and goes with the cream pumps on my feet. I carry a cream-colored clutch purse to match and a minimal pendant and pearl earrings.

Classy and simple, all ready to break up with my fake boyfriend in front of his family.

I hail a cab and get in. The cab driver asks for the address and I give him. He does a double-take in the rearview mirror.

I roll my eyes and look out the window. Surely, he knows whose home I'm headed to. Probably wondering what someone like me has to do with people like them.

Hopefully, by this time tomorrow, the Island and everyone here would be a past life I won't be revisiting anytime soon.

All their cars are outside once I get there. I'm the last one here. Great.

I check my phone and make sure I'm still on time. I am.

I climb up the steps to the door and ring the doorbell.

Please, anyone but Chance.

Sadly, my prayers go unanswered. Or more rightly, answered by a god who hates me.

Chance opens the door. He's in a patterned shirt and jeans with boots. I sweep my gaze over him making sure to avoid his eyes.

He sighs as if that bothers him. "Come in."

I skirt past him. The other person I see is Baxter. My smile is wide. "Hello! We meet again." I stretch my arms and he holds me in a hug.

He pulls away and looks over me. "You look too good for a Sunday dinner. I'm jealous." He glances over my shoulder, a smile in his eyes.

Both Chance and I don't address that. By the end of tonight, there'd be nothing to be jealous about. We'd be over.

"You look amazing yourself."

"That's my MO." He bows. "Can't do different."

"Oh, I know." I slip my hand around the curve of his elbow. He lifts his arm seamlessly, giving me a handhold. "Where's everyone?"

"Eager, aren't you?" He beams, pride in his eyes.

If only he knows I'm trying to escape his brother. I'd take the entire Easton clan over Chance right now.

"Aunt Felicia and Lucy are in the kitchen. Dad's choosing the wine with Landon." He starts off. "Come on. The kitchen's most interesting."

Aunt Felicia beams as we walk in. "Maddie, my dear. We have missed you coming around." She wipes her hands on her apron and comes to blow air kisses beside my cheeks. "Come, sit."

"I was thinking I could help?"

She ushers me to a stool by the island. "What? No way. Not when you're looking like a princess."

"Maybe I should dress up too, then I won't have to slice shit." Lucy eyes her mother as she chops carrots.

Aunt Felicia shakes her head. "Even if you're wearing the crown jewels, you'll still do your tasks."

Lucy walks past me. "Lucky," she whispers, then she pauses. "You smell good."

A blush heats my cheeks. "Thank you. And you—hmm."

She laughs. "I look a mess, I know." She shrugs. "I'll clean up before dinner, I promise."

I smile back. My eyes stray and fall on Chance. He stands by the door, looking half in, half out.

I swallow and look away, catching Baxter's gaze. His eyes narrow and he looks between Chance and me.

"Aunt Felicia," I say a little too loudly. "I should help."

She sighs. "Fine, if you insist."

I climb off the stool and stand next to her.

"You'll taste." She scoops a bit of sauce and holds it out to me.

The taste hits my tongue and I can't help my sigh.

"Delicious!"

She smiles and gives me more to taste. Even though I'm occupied, I see Baxter inch toward Chance and speak to him in a low voice. I can't make out what they're saying, but they look in my direction often. And once, Chance meets my eyes. The look in his eyes causes me to sputter.

"It's bad?" Aunt Felicia looks alarmed.

"No, it's good." I focus on her. "Very good. Just spicy." That much is true.

"Then it's perfect." She drops the ladle. "We're all done."

I look up and Chance is gone, just Baxter is left. His eyes carry a look I can't decipher.

Thankfully, Aunt Felicia gets in the way of whatever that is.

"Set the table, Baxter." She takes off her apron. "Lucy and I will go get ready."

They both leave and then I'm alone with Baxter.

I don't like the look he's giving me. "I can help set the table."

I start to pick up the stacked dishes but Baxter catches my hands. His bigger ones swallow mine, warm and solid.

"Maddie."

I meet his gaze. "What?"

He frowns. "Is something wrong?"

I shake my head. "No, why would you ask that?"

"Just an energy between you and Chance. Did something happen?" He glances at the door.

"No."

"Did he hurt you? I can beat his bossy ass up."

"God, no." I press a hand to my face. "He wouldn't do that."

"I know." He smiles. "Just want to be sure."

I smile as big as I can to assure him. "I swear. I'm fine."

He nods and releases my hand, pulling back. "Let's get these dishes out then, shall we?"

He takes a stack and heads out. I stare after him, my eyes filling up.

They're all so precious. I won't just be breaking up with Chance. I'll be hurting the entire family, but I have to. The longer this fake relationship stretches out, the more it'll hurt. And our time is up anyway. Best to rip the band-aid off in the cleanest way possible.

Baxter returns and frowns. Quickly, I pick up the dishes and ease past him.

When I have a moment alone, I dab away the moisture in my eyes.

Thankfully, everyone is ready soon after and there's no more time for me to wallow.

Everyone takes their seats and naturally, I'm placed next to Chance. My skin prickles with awareness. I can feel him, even though I keep my gaze on Dan. I don't allow the conversation to stall, asking everyone more questions. Never allowing it to slip to a subject that includes me and Chance.

Only when we're done with the main course do I look at Chance. He's with a glass of champagne, choosing to skip dessert.

He meets my eyes and his chest moves with a resigned sigh.

There's no backing out now. We have to do this.

How to start though...

I finish up my dessert and everyone's having a glass of wine and still chatting easily. I take my glass and reach for the bottle. A drink would help me work up the nerve.

But as my fingers close around the neck of the bottle, Chance's hand covers mine.

A warm thrill works through my body. I ignore the feeling and snatch my hand back, dislodging his hold a bit. Disquiet falls over everyone as they glance in our direction.

My first instinct is to play it off, but I pause that thought. This is the best time to break things off, now we have everyone's attention organically.

"You always do that," I whisper harshly.

"Do what?" His brows pull together.

"Always butting into my business with your fake chivalry." Chance looks confused. I almost sigh with exasperation. "You know, controlling me. I can't do this anymore."

He gets it then and his eyes spark with understanding. "Maddie, calm down. We can talk about it."

"No, no way! I'm done. It's over. We're through."

I start to rise, but he catches my arm.

"You can't mean that?"

The dinner table is so quiet I can hear my heartbeat. I search Chance's eyes. What is he doing? This is the part where he says 'Go if you want, I don't give a fuck.' But his soft, pleading gaze is nearly breaking me.

"I do. I can't be with you anymore. I've got to move on."

His jaw trembles. Is he hurt?

I force myself up. If I don't, I'll probably take my words back and that's far from the plan.

He rises with me and blocks my path. "I know you have to do this."

"We," I bite out, looking up into his hurt eyes. "We..." *agreed*. Why is he making this so hard?

"I made mistakes. I lied—"

"That's not what this is about," I bite out. "Just let me go."

"No." He holds my arms in a firm grip and pets the spots where the men manhandled me with gentle thumbs.

Tears cloud my eyes at his tenderness. "Why are you doing this?"

"You have to know." His voice is tight. "I never meant to hurt you. I messed up and I cannot take it back at this point, but I—" He exhales and shuts his eyes tightly before meeting mine again. "I want you to know that you've changed me for the better. It was a reckless decision... Trying to control you in the beginning. That wasn't fair and I'll always regret that. But since the moment I saw you struggling in the elevator..."

A sob breaks from my throat and a tear runs down my face.

"In your adorable non-dress and your scared eyes, I knew I wanted to be there for you. I wanted to fix everything that goes wrong around you. I don't know why." He runs a tender finger down my cheek. "It's what I've lived for every moment of the past three weeks. It's brought me more satisfaction than I've ever felt."

He pulls in a breath. "And I wish there was a better ending to this time with you. But I guess my fuckups were too much to forgive. Too grievous to let go."

No. My heart breaks, over and over. *I want you. For real. Please.*

"So I have to let you go."

I drop my gaze, unable to bear the hurt look in his eyes.

"I've lost you," he chokes out. "I have to regret that I did all the wrong things and made that happen, but it's okay. I'll hold this time in my heart forever."

He cups my cheek and presses a kiss on my forehead.

My body shakes as I cry, pressing my face against his chest. He hugs me tightly and works his hand into my hair as if he can hold me there forever.

I pull away and take a deep breath. "Goodbye, Chance."

His eyes shutter and his gaze drops. I resist the urge to cup his cheek and kiss him, ease his hurt, but that'll only worsen our pain. And confuse his family.

I wipe my eyes and turn to face them. The shock on their faces nearly makes me start bawling. I bite the inside of my cheek. "Goodbye, everyone."

Then my eyes meet Baxter's. He's not shocked, just very angry.

Chin trembling, I turn away and race out of the Eastons' home.

Chapter Twenty-Eight

Chance

I stare out the window. It's a muggy day. The sky is heavy with gray clouds and the sun is hidden. Raindrops beat against the glass but no actual rain.

A heavy sigh fills my chest and I let it out. My shoulders sink and the ball of dread in my stomach falls lower.

It's over. I should return to my work, but I can't.

This morning, I gave the go-ahead for Maddie to get paid. I came to terms with the fact that it is over.

Doing that sucked the life out of me. Last night was symbolic, but the raw truth lives in the day. She's not here. She would return home and I'd continue... existing without her.

I turn away from the window and look around the office. I lock myself away here to do my work—my most prized room. Yet, it looks like an architect's rendition.

No character, no style—flat and bleak, like me.

Maddie was my spark. My light. A flame burning bright in my dark world.

And now she's gone.

I'm nothing.

The lock turns and footsteps follow. Baxter. Coming to throw jabs at my stupidity? Well, he's welcome.

I have no defenses today.

I drop into my chair, my head bowed. "Make it quick. Take your time. Whatever. I don't care. Just be done and get out." I sound disembodied, like I'm not here, but miles into a dark, soulless abyss.

"I know you're hurting." The visitor's chair creaks as it absorbs his weight. "I know it's hard. I saw you both break down last night. And I can't pretend to know what truly went on between you both, but I know for sure you cared for each other deeply."

"I loved her." The words leave my mouth before I can think them through. And when I do think, I repeat, "I love her. With everything in me."

I raise my gaze to meet my brother's eyes.

"And now she's gone. I have nothing."

"Don't say that." He sits forward and places a hand on my folded ones. "You have us, but best of all, you have the memories between you both."

I scoff and look toward the plain gray wall. "And that's supposed to be comforting? It's nothing. Just three fucking weeks of my entire life! I wanted her—" My throat closes and the words can't escape. "I wanted her to stay."

I cannot bear to see what Baxter thinks about that. I go to the window and look out. The drizzle comes more steadily now.

"I... I don't know what to do." I pull in a breath that doesn't fill my lungs. "What the fuck do I do?"

Baxter's voice is little more than a whisper. "I always thought you'd tell her you loved her sooner, convince her to stay—"

"I'm not good for her, Bax. After Mom died, I gave up on myself. I became someone I don't recognize. Only when she came did I start to reconsider. See there's a different way to live."

Her words play in my head.

"She believes I can straighten up my act and be good for someone else. But not her and not now." I look up to the ceiling and breathe in, just to stem the moisture building behind my eyes. "If I told her then, and she said no, it's all lost. There's no hope, but if I can be better maybe—"

"You don't understand, do you?" Baxter rises, coming closer. "She cared—fuck it. She loved you with all your issues. The only reason she's bugging you about getting better is because she already cares."

I start to shake my head.

His hand clasps my shoulder. "Stop with the excuses. She does love you. Even with all your flaws." His voice drops. "As we all do."

I do a one-eighty to face him. We stand head to head, shoulder to shoulder. His gaze bores into mine, firm with conviction.

"We've never asked you to be anything but who you are. We just want you to be better. Same as her."

"You think so?"

He nods firmly.

My chest fills with hope, but to what end? Maddie must be up and away now. If I can find her though...

His lips twitch with a sad smile. "Should have had this talk before last night, right?"

"Should have."

"Take care, champ." Baxter claps my shoulder once, then leaves.

I'm alone once more. My heart feels too heavy for my chest, and I'm exhausted.

I drop back into my seat. Best to get on with work, right? That's the best distraction I can get now.

I flip open my laptop. An email pops in from Julia. It's about the leftover tasks that Maddie had yet to complete.

I'm hit with a wave of pain. By now, she'd have sashayed into my office, going over my calendar. She'd look like the brightest morning star and I'd be forced to keep my mind on task, remembering that she's my employee.

A knock sounds on the door then Julia walks in.

"Mr. Easton." She stops before me. "Here are your tasks for the day."

I stretch my hand. "Just give it."

She frowns, then hands over the paper. "Is there anything else you'd like? Since Maddie is gone, I can clear my schedule and take the minutes of meetings for you. I've booked a hotel for your trip next week. Maddie already RSVP'd so that's covered. If Maddie—"

"Just stop."

"What?" She stares at me wide-eyed.

"Stop saying her name."

Her mouth opens and shuts. "Um, okay... She—"

"Doesn't work either." I palm my face and run my fingers through my hair. "Can we do this later?"

I can't bear to be reminded every five seconds that Maddie was here. And now she's gone.

"Sir, if I may?"

"You may not."

"It's about Maddie."

"Then definitely don't."

"It's a good one."

"Julia," I sigh, falling back against my seat. By the look on her face, she won't be deterred. "Fine, go on." *Torture me.*

"Maddie's plane hasn't left yet."

A lump forms in my throat. I look away. "What is that to me, Julia?"

She huffs. "You and Maddie are the most stubborn—"

My eyes meet hers and she presses out a smile.

"Sorry. Just got ahead of myself there." She clears my throat. "All I'm saying is… the plane leaves by noon so you've got"—she glances at her watch—"two hours to get to her."

I keep my gaze steady, not betraying the hope building in my chest.

"If you want to get her back." She shrugs. "As an employee, of course."

I ignore her snarky tone and focus on the message—get Maddie back. Can I? If I show up at the airport, would she accept me? Last night, she was pretty clear she was done. And today, she left without even saying a final goodbye.

If that's not a clear message, I don't know what is.

"I've heard you, Julia." I look down at my laptop. "You can get back to work."

I lift my gaze in time to see her aghast look, and how she stomps out.

Chapter Twenty-Nine

Maddie

I'm sitting in the lounge next to other excited travelers. I don't mean to eavesdrop but it's hard not to catch their excited conversation. They relive their experiences on Magic Island and promise to come back sometime in the future.

Me? I sink lower in my seat and pray to all that's good and holy that the plane takes off soon. I want out of here.

Everything in me is itching to be back at the office. Or at the villa. Anywhere but at the airport. In only three weeks, I've grown attached to the Island.

My mind flashes to all the people I've met and become friends with. But the one that wrenches me the most is Chance.

I'm still teary-eyed from last night's dinner. I dab my face and hope no one notices.

I'm a grown woman. I shouldn't be crying over a man I know isn't available. But I can't help it. He made his choice, and I made mine.

It's over for us.

But I don't want it to be. My heart squeezes with a persistent ache. I should have gone to the office to say a last goodbye. Even though the relationship was a sham, he was a great boss. He was a great man.

I just can't stand seeing him and not being able to touch him.

I suck in a breath and push it out. It's still an hour till boarding.

Fuck.

"Maddie?"

I sit up, sure I'm imagining the sound of my name.

"Maddie!"

I turn and my eyes grow wide. Chance stands at the doorway to the lounge. An airport staff has his metal detector out, blocking him.

When our eyes connect, he shoves the man out of the way and hurries for me. I rise, unable to pull in a full breath. Numerous questions tumble in my head, but I'm unable to get even one out.

Chance rushes to stop before me. He cups my face, somber eyes taking me in.

"What are you doing here?" I whisper, but it's almost a shout.

The place is suddenly quiet, everyone focused on us. Even the staff stands back, not interrupting.

"I couldn't bear to let you leave without letting you know," his voice is hoarse.

My heart flips in my chest. I fist his jacket to steady my shaking. "There's nothing to say now."

"No," he breathes and cups my face, thumbing my cheeks. "I have to. I—" He gulps. "I'm sorry, Maddie. I wasn't sincere with you. I should have been. I was just afraid."

"Afraid?"

He nods. "I should have told you sooner. I should have told you I only started living when you came into my life. Nothing had meaning until I met you. That you make everything better and brighter and I can't let you go now. Not after I've seen what life can be with you in it."

Gooseflesh breaks out on my arms. My breath gasps out of me. "Chance, what are you saying?"

"I'm saying I love you, Maddie. I love you with all my heart." He tilts my face, looking into my eyes as if he's seeing something he never has before. "I can't let you leave. Not like this. I want you here with me."

I sniff back the tears trying to escape my eyes. "You... I..." A sob breaks from my throat.

He hugs me briefly, letting me calm down. When he pulls back, his blue eyes glow with hope, with a plea. "What do you say, Maddie?"

"Do you want me back as your assistant?"

He frowns. "No, no. Of course not. You're more than that to me. That was only an excuse to get close to you."

"So..." I swallow a breath. "Who will I be to you then if I stay?"

His lips twitch. "Will you be my girlfriend? For real?"

Peace threads through my being, filling my limbs. "You mean that?"

"Every word, Maddie." He runs a thumb down my chin. "Remain on Magic Island. Be my girlfriend."

"Yes," I say on a breath. There's no other answer. This is all I've wanted—for Chance to be mine, and me, his. "I'll stay."

He exhales, his chest caving, then he yanks me against him. His mouth comes down on mine, deep and searching.

Applause rises around us, but I don't pay it any mind. I'm kissing Chance for the first time, knowing that this is real. We are together.

And it feels good. It's the best feeling ever.

I rise on my tiptoes and loop my arms around his neck, wanting more of him. He indulges me, sweeping his tongue into my mouth and mixing our tastes.

Our kiss is tainted with my salty tears, but more than that, there's love and security.

A whoop goes up and brings me back to the present. We're still standing in the airport lounge.

I pull away and Chance grins.

"Can we go now?" he asks.

I grin. "Of course."

We get my luggage and leave the airport together.

Chance doesn't return to work. He takes me to his home instead. He walks us past the guest bedroom to his master bedroom, and he deposits my luggage next to the closet.

"There's enough room for the both of us." He looks around the space, his brows drawn.

He's so serious a smile tugs on my lips. "I don't remember the part where I agreed to move in with you."

He spins my way, his eyes wide, probably worried he has goofed. When he sees my smile, he chuckles and comes over to kiss my lips tenderly. "Yeah, well. I'm bossy that way."

"Ugh." I roll my eyes. "What did I get myself into?"

"A good time." He kisses my jaw and nips at my earlobe.

His hands slip up my hips to my back, pulling me against him, letting me feel every inch of him.

I shut my eyes and drown in the sensation. I can't quite believe it. Minutes ago, I was at the airport, leaving him behind, leaving *this* behind. I had no hope. But now?

I brush back his hair and look into his eyes. "I love you, Chance."

He smiles and kisses me slowly. "I love you, too."

Chapter Thirty

Maddie

My office overlooks the city. The first time I walked into it, I ran to the glass and looked out the window, marveling.

"For me?" I squealed.

"Yep," Ramsey responded. "Right next to mine." He shot an accusing glare Chance's way.

Chance simply shrugged. "What do you think?"

"I love it!" I could barely keep from hopping in one spot.

Even though it's half of Chance's and was covered in dust from lack of use, it was mine. I spent the next week cleaning up, decorating, and giving it character.

Right now, it's a playful purple and pink with pretty artworks on the walls. I have a sitting area with two couches and a cute little coffee table.

The space brings me joy.

Not today, though.

Right now, I'm neck-deep in work and I have zero time to admire my handiwork. Being the new co-lead of the marketing department means I have a lot to live up to for my first campaign. And it's a drag.

Now, I understand why Ramsey's always grumpy.

At first, when Chance appointed me in this position, the man griped, but two weeks later, he started to warm up to me. And now, we're doing great—if that means being civil to each other.

I've always suspected he's fine with me taking the position because he doesn't have to be under scrutiny all by himself now. And boy, do we get some serious scrutiny.

It doesn't matter that Chance and I carpool to work and back home every day. When we're here, it's all business and he calls me out the way he does any of his other employees.

Hell, I once mentioned I'd rather go back to being just his PA because he used to give me some slack then. He frowned thoughtfully, but I kissed that thought away. I love my new position.

Plus, he has a new PA to take care of his tasks. It's a step in the right direction for him since he's easing back on being so tied to his work.

Wait, where was I?

Yes, we have to establish a committee that would take care of monitoring the progress of the campaign. I type this down, then scroll up to go over my notes again.

There's a knock at the door and the lock turns. I look up.

Long legs covered in warm brown slacks step into the office. My lips curve into a smile as I let my gaze sweep up his frame to his face.

Chance lifts a brow, a smile in his eyes. "What?"

"Nothing." I shrug. "You're just a sight for sore eyes."

He tsks as he rounds my desk to stand behind me. "Stressed?" He palms my shoulders and massages away the kink in my neck.

"Mm-hmm." I shut my eyes and bow my head, opening up for more of his touch.

He chuckles lightly and leans in to kiss my nape.

A shudder rushes through me and I bite back a moan.

"Is it good?" he rumbles against my ear.

"Very." I adjust in my seat, giving my center some much-needed friction.

"I saw that." He kisses my nape again.

"I wanted you to." I raise my head and his hands fall off, then I spin around so I'm facing him.

My dress is caught around my mid-thighs and I widen my legs. His eyes catch on the movement and his eyes darken.

"Here for a mid-morning snack, Mr. Easton?"

His throat bobs.

I've got him.

I reach for his belt buckle, for sure he's going to let me, but he catches my hands.

"That's not why I'm here." His voice is strained like that's the last thing he wants to say.

"Then why are you here?" I flip my hair over one shoulder, baring my neck.

Chance grins and looks away. "Stop tempting me."

"Come on. You're hard enough to fuck through steel." I palm the tent in his slacks and he moves away. "Let's just steal a moment."

"No, really, we can't." His eyes take on a warm light. "You have to come with me. There's a surprise waiting for you."

My brows furrow. "Really?"

"I swear it."

"And where is this thing?"

"Is it a thing?" He scrunches up his face adorably. "I don't know. But you'll know when you see."

"Chance," I warn, rising to my feet and adjusting my dress. "This better be good."

He adjusts his hard-on. "I promise, it is." He leans in and smacks a kiss on my cheek. "I won't dare play a prank when you're this horny."

"What do you mean by *this horny*?" I gasp. "You were the one that touched me first."

He places a hand on my lower back and guides me to the door. "And you responded."

"Yes, because you started it."

"You could have easily just said no."

His tone is playful but I'm a mite pissed. "You know what? I'm saying no to you tonight."

We break out into the corridor and he leans in to whisper in my ear. "You most certainly won't."

A shiver slices through me and my breath hitches. "I will. Watch me."

I prance off, leaving him in my wake.

"Oh, I'm definitely watching."

I turn around to find him staring at my backside. "You don't get that either!" I hurry back and nudge him forward, coming up behind him. "Now go show me this surprise you have for me."

Some staff we walk past keep their gazes ahead, while others glance in our direction with a smile. It's no secret now that we're a couple.

After three months, I'm certain the whole building knows it. And it's not like we're great at hiding it, or even trying to.

Chance kisses me every opportunity he gets and no matter who's around. It pleases me to know he's not ashamed of us, so I clasp my hand around his elbow every time we're walking next to each other.

We round a corner to the main area of the floor when I come to a gasping halt. My hands fly to my mouth as I stare at the scene before me.

My dad, mom and Natalie stand next to Julia, chatting about heaven knows what. All I do know is that my eyes are filling up and I can't breathe.

I turn to Chance. "You didn't."

His smile is pleased. "Let's go say hi."

Halfway there, I scream, "Mom, Dad!"

Mom rushes forward and hugs me tightly. "My baby, I've missed you so, so much."

Dad squeezes us both. "So good to see you, kiddo."

I breathe in their scents and feel their comforting warmth. "How on earth are you two here?"

After deciding to remain on Magic Island, I wanted to see my family and Nat, but work at the company kept me from leaving. I promised myself I'd leave once the campaign was underway.

And now they're here!

I pull away to draw Natalie into a hug. "I missed you so much."

She holds me tight. "I missed you too, babe."

I stand back and look over their smiling faces. "Now someone, tell me how this is possible! I'm dying."

"Don't say that, love," Mom chides.

"People who are dying don't announce it," Dad adds.

I laugh until my eyes fill up, then I wipe at them.

"Chance contacted me saying that he'd like to bring your parents over since you missed them," Nat explains. "So I asked and they were game, so here we are."

I spin to face Chance. Unable to hold back, I palm his face and kiss him with all the love growing in my heart. When I pull away, my parents are looking at me expectantly.

"Mom, Dad, meet Chance Easton, my boyfriend." I thread my fingers through his. "And Chance, these are my parents, Mr. and Mrs. Lowe."

As they exchange greetings, I feel my heart fill up. All the people I care for are here, what more can I ask for?

Much more, apparently.

Chance had a whole family dinner planned. Mine and his. All together on one table.

He picked an outdoor restaurant, and at seven p.m., we are all gathered underneath the setting sun.

Dan clicks his silverware on his glass and draws everyone's attention. His speech about treasuring moments like this warms my heart.

I look over at the group. Dan and my dad are wrapped up in a conversation. My mom and Aunt Felicia are bonding over their love for cooking. Lucy and Natalie are talking, occasionally pointing to Natalie's hair. Baxter's caught in a one-sided conversation with Landon.

Me and Chance? I turn left to meet his eyes. He's staring at me with the softest look that sends a shiver through me.

"Cold?" He frowns.

I'm not, but he's already tugging off his jacket. It's off him when something falls out of the inner pocket.

He bends and his head hits the underside of the table. "Shit."

"I'll get it." I stand and crouch.

"No, don't!"

Why does he sound alarmed? I know it's unladylike to be crouched in an evening gown as I am but no one cares, I'm sure.

I grab the... velvet box and pause. I meet Chance's eyes. He grimaces.

"Wh—" I swallow my thoughts. I can't jump to conclusions. Not until I see what it is for sure.

I come up with the box and he reaches for it even before I can get a look.

"Hey!" I keep it out of his reach, raised over my head.

His brows draw down. "Give it back."

Now, everyone's watching us.

"No. I picked it off the floor fair and square."

"Maddie." He reaches for me again.

I kick back the seat and jump out of the way. He doesn't stop coming after me. I run around the table to the delight of our families.

"Go, Maddie," Baxter cheers. "Don't give it back!"

Chance shoots his brother a glare before looking back at me with a plea in his eyes.

I've managed to keep four chairs between us this entire time. "Just let me see it, then I'll stop."

"No, you can't—"

I pop the box open. A diamond ring winks at me. Everyone sees it too because we all fall silent.

My heart thuds. I look up to meet his eyes.

"I was going to propose," he says slowly. Then his gaze drops. "I guess I botched it."

Love for him fills my chest. "No, you haven't."

I walk over to where he stands. It takes some maneuvering since I'm in heels but eventually, I get down on one knee.

Chance's eyes twinkle. "What are you doing?"

"I guess since I have the ring," I hold the open box out to him. "I'm doing the asking. Will you marry me, Chance Easton?"

He laughs, shaking his head. "Of course, I will. But the question was yours to answer." He pulls me up. "Maddie, will you be my wife?"

"Yes."

Someone gasps and an uproar fills the air. Chance pulls me against himself, kissing me deeply.

He lets go and takes the ring, slipping it onto my finger. He only gives me a moment to admire it before he's drawing me up against his chest again.

"I love you," he whispers.

"I love you, Chance," I respond. "Now and always."

I'd be grateful if you'd share your thoughts on this story in an Amazon review.

REVIEW LINK: SCAN QR CODE

Please check the other books too from Summer's catalog below.

Receive a FREE BOOK and join Summer's mailing list.

About the author

Summer currently lives in Hawaii, which offers the best weather on the planet.

Besides the weather, she enjoys receiving inspiration from Hawaii's multicultural events and foods.

Her imagination grows beyond the Pacific Ocean and lands on readers' Kindle tablets.

She enjoys writing "Love, Spice, and Suspense. Always Happily Ever After" books.

Sing up for Summer's newsletter; https://dl.bookfunnel.com/7hdo5h20u8

She may send you some pictures she took in her neighborhood.

Aloha....

Printed in Dunstable, United Kingdom